"Do You Play?"

a husky voice asked.

Thomas Murphy turned his head to gaze down into big, dark eyes. Close up, Michelle DeMara didn't resemble a pool shark, but the expression on her pixie face meant business. "Do I play what?" he asked cautiously.

She nodded impatiently at the pool stick in Thomas's hand. "Pool. Do you play?"

"Occasionally," he said, fighting a smile. "I'm no Minnesota Fats, though. Are you looking for a game?"

She shrugged. "I'm just killing time."

"I hear your methods are brutal," he murmured. "I'm not sure I'm up to the challenge."

"We'll just play for fun."

She gave him one last smile and turned on her heel, walking back to the pool table with a rhythm that was enthralling. Thomas watched her, feeling as if his smile were becoming permanent. He had no idea how women walked in skirts that narrow; he was simply glad they did.

"Yeah. We're going to have *so* much fun," he murmured wickedly.

Dear Reader:

Happy New Year! 1991 is going to be a terrific year at Silhouette Desire. We've got some wonderful things planned, starting with another of those enticing, irresistible, tantalizing men. Yes, *Man of the Month* will continue through 1991!

Man of the Month kicks off with *Nelson's Brand* by Diana Palmer. If you remember, Diana Palmer launched *Man of the Month* in 1989 with her fabulous book, *Reluctant Father*. I'm happy to say that *Nelson's Brand* is another winner—it's sensuous, highly charged and the hero, Gene Nelson, is a man you'll never forget.

But January is not only *Man of the Month*. This month, look out for additional love stories, starting with the delightful *Four Dollars and Fifty-One Cents* by Lass Small. And no, I'm not going to tell you what the title means—you'll have to read the book! There's also another great story by Carole Buck, *Paradise Remembered,* a sexy adventure by Jean Barrett, *Heat,* and a real charmer from Cathie Linz, *Handyman*. You'll also notice a new name, Ryanne Corey. But I'm sure you'll want to know that she's already written a number of fine romances as Courtney Ryan. Believe me, *The Valentine Street Hustle* is a winner!

As for February... well, I can't resist giving you a peek into next month. Get ready for *Outlaw* by Elizabeth Lowell! Not only is this a *Man of the Month*, it's also another powerful WESTERN LOVERS series.

You know, I could go on and on... but I'll restrain myself right now. Still, I will say that 1991 is going to be filled with wonderful things from Silhouette Desire. January is just the beginning!

All the best,
Lucia Macro
Senior Editor

RYANNE COREY

THE VALENTINE STREET HUSTLE

SILHOUETTE *Desire*®

Published by Silhouette Books New York

America's Publisher of Contemporary Romance

SILHOUETTE BOOKS
300 East 42nd St., New York, N.Y. 10017

THE VALENTINE STREET HUSTLE

Copyright © 1991 by Tonya Wood

ISBN: 0-373-05615-X

First Silhouette Books printing January 1991

Printed in the U.S.A.

RYANNE COREY

loves to travel, but for the first few years of her marriage, the majority of her travel experiences consisted of trips to and from the hospital to have her children. Four boys and one girl later, she decided to broaden her horizons. Unfortunately, it seemed wherever she and her husband traveled, disaster followed. A trip to Mexico coincided with a hurricane. When they visited Hawaii, a volcano erupted. And yes, they visited San Francisco just before the earthquake.

Luckily, Ryanne has a good sense of humor. She says, "Life is entirely too serious to be taken seriously." And by far, the most important ingredient in her work is humor.

One

He couldn't take his eyes off her.

It wasn't that she sat alone at the bar, a long-legged blonde with an expensive pink leather jacket slung negligently over her shoulders. It wasn't the hectic glitter of diamonds at her ears, which had been triple-pierced. It wasn't the evocative, childlike curve shaping her wide, expressive mouth, or the faint dusting of freckles scattered over a small, straight nose. It wasn't even the tantalizing expanse of sun-kissed thigh revealed beneath her pencil-thin pink leather skirt.

It was the way she handled the peanuts.

She picked one up with her left hand, juggling it in the center of her palm for a second or two. Then suddenly she would slap the back of her hand, the peanut would go flying above her head and she would catch it in her mouth, neat as a pin. She never missed. And she never gave any indication she was aware of the curious stares she attracted from the patrons of Shenanigans Bar and Grill.

Thomas Murphy crossed his arms over his chest, his chair tipped back on two legs as he studied the blond peanut popper at the bar. Fascinating. Shenanigans often played host to the diamond-crusted upper class, but the upper class seldom possessed juggling skills.

A dark-haired waiter dropped in the chair opposite Thomas, propping his elbow on the table and his chin in his palm. "I think I'm in love," he said.

Thomas didn't have to look at him to know the direction of his gaze. Harry had a notorious soft spot for doe-eyed blondes. Both men watched another peanut sail into the air, eyes lifting and falling in perfect unison.

"You fall in love every night, Harry," Thomas replied absently.

"I do try," Harry said humbly, his lively gaze as deceptively sweet as an infant's. "As my esteemed employer often tells me, you only live once."

His esteemed employer grinned. "And if you do it right, pal, once around is all you need."

"Did you see that? Two peanuts at once. The girl has superb eye-hand coordination. I tell you, the mind boggles. What do you think she would do if I asked for her phone number?"

"I'll give you my studied opinion in about five seconds." Thomas watched as a well-dressed lounge lizard with drink in hand whispered something, his perfectly moussed head bent close to hers. She turned her head, staring him down with a wide-eyed gaze and the ghost of a mocking smile. It was incredible, Thomas thought. She couldn't have been more than eighteen or nineteen years old. No woman should have a look that intimidating at nineteen. Lord only knew what she would be capable of at twenty-five.

The lizard quickly moved to the far end of the bar and downed the last of his drink in one gulp. Harry turned to Thomas, wincing comically. "Ouch, ouch, ouch."

"Doesn't look promising, does it?" Thomas murmured. "You'll have to fall in love elsewhere tonight." He smiled and gave Harry his empty glass. "And wait until your break, buddy. Bring me another ginger ale in the meantime."

"I really hate not getting what I want," Harry mourned, trudging off into the smoky room.

Thomas watched the young woman for several minutes after Harry departed, bright-eyed and amused. He did appreciate a genuine nonconformist, though his appreciation was less predatory than Harry the waiter's. At thirty-four, Thomas was old enough to be her father. Well, not quite old enough, he amended after his healthy male ego demanded a quick calculation. But he was certainly old enough to know better than to fall under the spell of a sweet young thing with superb eye-hand coordination. More was the pity. There were definite disadvantages to being a somewhat mature and more or less responsible man.

Harry returned with his drink and an off-color joke he had just heard from the bartender. Thomas listened absently, his attention still focused on the young woman at the bar. She asked for the telephone and made a short call. She rebuffed another advance from a curly-haired preppie type with a fresh sunburn. She emptied the peanut dish, then took her drink and left the bar. Through the flickering candles on dozens of tables, Thomas followed the bright blond head as she moved through the shifting crowd.

"That was the punch line," Harry said, tapping Thomas on the shoulder.

Thomas nodded, watching her pause in front of the heavy mahogany doors that led to the billiard room. "Okay."

"You're not laughing."

"I'm laughing on the inside, Harry." She'd disappeared. He'd looked at Harry for three seconds and she'd just disappeared. Thomas couldn't imagine she would just walk into the game room. Only a few of the hard-core Saturday-night regulars even knew of its existence. From inside the restaurant, the doors appeared to lead to an office or a meeting room. Perhaps she was looking for the rest room...?

"So I'll work on my delivery," Harry grumbled, walking off.

Grinning, Thomas waited for Blondie to do a quick about-face through those double doors. Women were so predictable. You could count on the fragile darlings, one and all, to feel extremely uncomfortable in a billiard room. They disliked the heavy smoke, they didn't appreciate the boisterous humor and they didn't approve of the enthusiastic betting. A delicate woman-child in a trendy pink leather jacket would hardly feel at home in the big nasty poolroom.

He waited a full ten minutes, his gleeful amusement evaporating. He couldn't imagine what she was doing in there. He tried to remember who was playing tonight. Philip Sommerfield, the party-loving son of one of Rhode Island's old-money families, and a few of his college buddies. The Denehey brothers, who usually made a tidy sum hustling mediocre pool players like Sommerfield. Harmless enough types, if you didn't mind the blue language.

Curiosity and yet another joke from Harry finally drove him to the billiard room. He entered quietly, puzzled by the unusual silence. His gaze lit upon the crush of bodies gathered around the center table, his brows drawing together as he spotted a bright blond head. He couldn't see the table itself, but he recognized the crack of the cue ball, then the unmistakable sound of a pool ball dropping into a pocket.

The spectators broke into wild cheers, obviously amused by the outcome of the game. Everett Denehey shouldered his way through the crowd, two hard stains on his cheekbones and a cue stick in his hand. "Shortest damn game of nine ball I ever played," he growled to no one in particular.

"Damnedest thing I ever saw. Who would have thought? How the hell was I supposed to know?"

"How much did you lose?" Thomas asked, stifling a grin. Everett didn't believe in losing gracefully.

"Two hundred." Everett looked over his shoulder, pointing an accusing finger. "See that pretty little blonde over there, Murphy? Tell me, does Goldilocks look like a bleedin' pool shark to you? Usually I can spot a hustler, but, hell... *look* at her, Murphy."

Thomas was looking. The crowd had shifted, and Goldilocks was clearly visible. She had shed her pink jacket, and her breasts pressed softly against the white knit of her blouse. The fluorescent light drifted through her hair like a sun shower, and her dark-lashed eyes were merry. Her smile, directed at her male audience at large, was an equal mixture of innocence, satisfaction and amusement. "*She* beat you?" Thomas asked stupidly.

Everett nodded, gripping his cue stick in both hands as though he would like to snap it in half. "I'll never hear the end of it. I could handle losing money to one of the guys, but a fluffy blond thing... well, hell. It's damned humiliating." He gave Thomas the cue stick in an abrupt movement. "I need a beer."

Everett stomped through the doors leading back to the restaurant, his chunky body stiff as a rod. Thomas watched with a sympathetic smile, pitying any man who was taken for a bundle by a fluffy blond thing. Like the man said, it was damned humiliating. "Do you play?" a husky voice asked.

Thomas turned his head slowly, gazing down into big, dark eyes with a soft jolt of surprise. Close up, she didn't resemble a fluffy blond thing. Neither did she resemble a pool shark, but the expression on her pixie face meant business. "Do I play what?" he asked cautiously.

She nodded impatiently at the pool stick in Thomas's hand, her fine gold hair swinging in a glossy arc. "Pool. Do you play?"

Help, Thomas thought with a sudden wave of amusement. I'm being stalked by Bambi. "Occasionally," he said, fighting a smile. "I'm no Minnesota Fats, though. Are you looking for a game?"

She shrugged. "My car broke down outside. I called someone to pick me up, but it's going to be a while until he gets here. Till then, I'm just killing time."

"I hear your methods are brutal," he murmured, sparing a brief thought for poor Denehey. "I'm not sure I'm up to the challenge."

"So I'll spot you the eight ball," she replied generously.

Thomas's blue-eyed gaze began to sparkle. Talk about taking candy from a baby. "I don't know...I haven't played for a while." Not since seven o'clock that evening, actually, but who was keeping track? "I probably wouldn't be much competition for you."

"Okay." She sighed and pulled a face. "I'll spot you the break *and* the eight ball. You can't ask for more than that."

Such a confident fluffy blond thing. Thomas dropped his head to hide his giveaway smile. There were those—he thought of Denehey and Harry the waiter—who might be so taken in by sweet female curves and a baby-freckled nose that they missed the determined set of her chin and the canny light in her chocolate-bar eyes. With insight born of experience, Thomas recognized a self-assurance far beyond her tender years. Still...a little dose of humility was always beneficial for the young. "That really isn't necessary," he said, his voice quavering slightly.

"Listen, if you're worried about money, we'll just play for fun. No bets. Plus I'll spot you the—"

"There's no need for that." He stood very straight, squaring his shoulders, making it perfectly clear his male pride was at stake. "I'm sure I can handle a fair game and a little wager."

She looked doubtful. "It's fine with me if we just play for fun. I prefer it, to tell you the truth."

"I'll tell you what." He smiled sweetly, the edges of his mouth curling into charming tucks. Those who knew him well would have recognized that smile and slipped their wallets deeper into their pockets. "We'll play for...say, a million dollars a rack. How does that sound?"

Her eyes widened, then her nose crinkled and she began to laugh. Obviously she assumed he was teasing her, salving his pride with an outrageous bet neither of them would have to take seriously. "A million a rack? Are you sure you don't want to make it five or ten million?"

"Oh, I've never been a high roller," he said. "I'm a pretty conservative guy."

"Well, then...I don't see the harm in a little bet." Her voice was whimsical, indulgent. "All right. A million a rack, it is."

She gave him one last smile and turned on her heel, walking back to the pool table with a rhythm that was enthralling. Thomas watched her, his smile feeling as if it were becoming permanent. He had no idea how women walked in skirts that narrow; he was simply glad they did.

"We're going to have so much fun," he murmured wickedly.

By her calculations, he now owed her four million dollars.

Michelle DeMara chalked her cue, preparing to add yet another million to her fantasy winnings. The largely male audience gathered around the table had gradually increased in the past thirty minutes, with most of the men wearing identical expressions of mute ecstasy. Apparently her opponent had beaten nearly everyone in the room at one time or another, and his downfall was being observed with great relish. Michelle still wasn't sure just what his name was, since they had never bothered to formally introduce themselves. She had heard him called Murphy, Tommy, Thomas Bud, Murphy Babe and Poor Bugger by the amused spectators. She had heard herself referred to as Honey, Baby Doll, Sugar and Blondie. The names didn't bother her. Michelle was no stranger to a billiard room, and "Blondie" was fairly tame compared to the names she would have been called—and had been called in the past—at less respectable establishments. Shenanigans Bar and Grill was one of the most popular watering holes in all of Newport. She felt as comfortable here as she would have felt at the Monday-night bingo game at Saint Peter and Paul Church. More comfortable, actually.

The room grew hushed as she took her position at the table. Almost absently she called her shot: "Eight ball, corner pocket." It was a difficult bank shot, but one she had made successfully hundreds of times before. She wasn't nervous. She wouldn't even have been nervous if she had actually been playing for such a staggering amount of money. A highly unorthodox upbringing was greatly responsible for her ironclad composure. There weren't many babies who learned to walk hanging on to the edge of a pool table. She was at home here, with the drifting smoke and the hot lights and the steady level of pressure. Then again—she shrugged almost imperceptibly as she drew back her cue stick—she was at home almost anywhere.

The room froze, remained that way for a silent moment as she made her shot. The eight ball dropped neatly into the corner pocket, and Michelle DeMara was a million dollars richer. So to speak.

Grinning, she walked over to Murphy Babe and offered him her hand. The expression on his face was priceless: *Superior Male Has Painful Identity Crisis.* She'd realized early on in the game that the man had tried to hustle her. He was a superb player, nearly as good as she, but not quite.

"You owe me five million dollars," she said.

He shook her hand, his wide mouth twisted in self-derision. "I hope you take American Express."

He lost with flair, she had to give him that. It couldn't have been easy for him. Murphy Babe was well into his thirties, and his seasoned manner belonged to a man who was accustomed to making his own rules. For the first time since the game began, she allowed herself to concentrate completely on her vanquished opponent. His gold-on-brown hair was thick and ribbon shiny, a silky, disheveled mane that completely covered his collar in the back. His expressive features held the telltale marks of sun and smiles, a network of tiny lines radiating from the corners of his bright silver-blue eyes, deeper grooves curving around his wide mouth. She could see a small muscle twitching in his hard brown cheek, possibly a side effect of losing five million dollars to a mere woman. Other than that, he seemed to be in fairly good spirits.

All in all, a worthy opponent, she decided impishly, indulging a natural feminine appreciation of the hard, flowing muscles that gave beautiful shape to faded denims and a simple white shirt. Cocky, but in an endearing sort of way. That wounded "how could you?" look on his expressive face when she had made that crucial bank shot was quite touching. She was almost sorry she hadn't given him the last game. Almost.

"Fortunately for you," she said, "I offer thirty-year loans at the going interest rate. With approved credit."

He looked at her, then at his grinning audience. "Denehey was right," he said. "This is damned humiliating."

"I don't suppose you'd like to play another..."

He looked startled. "No. Hell, no."

"Oh. Well, thanks. It was fun." She sighed, then retrieved her jacket from the back of a nearby chair. It was useless to try and find someone else to play her. Not a single frightened male chauvinist in the entire room would meet

her eyes. They were laughing and slapping Murphy Babe on
the back and nonchalantly migrating toward the doors. Why
couldn't men simply look upon women as equals? Why was
it perfectly acceptable to lose to a male, but downright humiliating to lose to a female? Michelle wouldn't mind losing to a man . . . should that unlikely event ever occur.

A wide path opened up for her as she left the room. She
couldn't remember the last time she had spooked a group of
hardened pool players quite like this. A heavyset, red-haired
bear of a man with an anchor tattooed on his arm held the
doors open for her, smiling stiffly and staring at the floor.
She wondered what would happen if she whispered "Boo!"
in his ear, then decided against it. Male pride had taken
enough of a beating tonight.

She found a quiet table in the corner of the restaurant and
ordered a soft drink. Apparently the word had spread
quickly among Shenanigans' regulars that she was a dangerous and unscrupulous woman. Although a few curious
glances were thrown her way, not once did anyone attempt
to speak to her besides the waiter, and even he had a wary
light in his eyes. Michelle passed the time burning toothpicks in the candle flame and dropping the charred slivers
in the ashtray—a miniature toothpick graveyard. She'd wait
another five minutes and call a cab if Sam didn't show up.
After the excitement of a five-million-dollar pool game,
toothpick burning left her cold.

When she ran out of toothpicks, she let her gaze travel
over the room, absorbing the atmosphere, the sounds, the
colors. A strange prickling on the back of her neck made her
suddenly turn her head and she saw Murphy Babe sitting
alone at a table at the far side of the room. He was staring
at her with those Newman-blue eyes, just . . . staring at her.
A whisper of a smile passed over his lips, and she had the
impression he was smiling at himself rather than at her.

For a quiet moment her heart beat strangely as their gazes
held, then she looked away. For the first time that night, she

wasn't entirely comfortable. Her throat was a little dry, and the room felt too warm. She plucked at the clinging white material of her blouse, wishing she'd worn something cooler. Wishing that Sam would come. Wondering if she'd given him the right address on Valentine Street.

A shadow fell over her, blocking the light and the scant breeze from the overhead ceiling fan. Murphy Babe leaned both hands on the tabletop, his golden-brown hair falling forward in a silky tangle. "Do you mind if I ask you something?" he said politely.

Michelle shrugged and picked up her drink, ignoring the tattered heartbeats that spilled into her throat. "I suppose that depends on the question."

He sat down without being invited, raising the heel of his shoe to rest on the table's heavy pedestal base. His expression was thoughtful as he nodded toward the glass in her hand. "Are you old enough to be drinking that?"

"Gosh." She gave a soft laugh and began to breathe again. Her scattered wits were still romping like kittens in clover, but at least she had oxygen. "I don't know. How old do you have to be in Rhode Island to drink a soft drink?"

"Oh." His eyes tucked at the corners with a rueful smile. He leaned back in his chair, hooking his arms behind his neck. "So humor me. If that was a martini instead of a soft drink, would you be old enough to drink it?"

Michelle's head tipped against her shoulder as she looked at him. Her dark eyes were wide, thoughtful and almost innocent. "Would it bother you," she said slowly, "if you lost five million dollars to a minor?"

He paled slightly, his smile dropping off at one corner. "A minor? Are you trying to tell me you're—"

She nodded. "A sixteen-year-old pool shark."

There was a moment of perfect silence. Michelle waited. Murphy Babe stared at her, the numb astonishment in his expression gradually giving way to reluctant amusement. He leaned toward her in deliberate slow motion, his forearms resting on the table, his sun-browned face only inches from hers. Candlelight picked out the faint, self-mocking lines of his smile. "You know, you're really good," he said softly. "A dangerous combination of Shirley Temple and Lizzie Borden. How old are you, brown eyes?"

For a moment she couldn't remember. Murphy Babe's husky voice was a sudden assault on her senses, making her feel strange and fragile and vaguely threatened all at once. She pushed herself backward against her chair, a tiny frown etched between her brows. "I'm twenty-four," she said, her voice sounding sharper than she'd intended. Then, at his patently incredulous look, "It's true. I can't help it if I look younger than I really am. It's the curse of my life, believe me."

Twenty-four, Thomas thought. What a nice surprise. "Oh, I imagine it's quite an advantage when you're hustling a game of pool."

His words brought her chin up. "I'm not a pool hustler."

"No?"

"No."

"Okay. We'll let that go for now." He sat back in his chair, amusement rimming the wide corners of his wayward mouth. "So tell me...where did you learn to play pool like that?"

Michelle was much more comfortable with the width of the table between them, though she still felt as though there wasn't quite enough air in the room. "Just a little something I learned at my daddy's knee," she replied, striving for a lighter tone.

"Daddy must have been some pool player," he murmured, his curious gaze wandering from her eyes to her blond hair to the clusters of diamonds at her ears. "You certainly don't look like any pool shark I've come up against before. Do you have a real name, or should I just call you Fats, Jr.?" Then, when she glared at him, he added quickly,

"After Minnesota Fats, the great pool player. The two of you have quite a bit in common."

As a matter of fact, there had been a time in her dimpled childhood when her nickname had been "Baby Fats." Michelle preferred to keep that her little secret. "You probably mean that as a compliment," she replied, her eyes daring him to contradict her.

He gave her a crooked half smile. "Hmm. Probably. *My* name is Thomas Alexander Murphy, and I've never met anyone like you in my life. You juggle peanuts. That's rare. Besides, you have an interesting attitude."

She smiled stiffly. "I don't believe anyone's ever admired my attitude before."

"Oh, they have, believe me. Among other things. For instance, you don't simper, cringe or hesitate."

"Neither does Rambo," she said, less than thrilled.

"Also you've been sitting in a room surrounded by mirrors for the past fifteen minutes, and you haven't glanced at yourself once. It's hardly the kind of thing you would expect from someone with your looks. So, Fats..." He changed the subject with a shrug and a brilliant, whimsical smile. "How do we handle this little debt I owe you? How about ten dollars a week at seven percent? Should I put it on paper so everything's legal?"

"My name is not Fats."

"Then what is your name, sugar lips?" an unfamiliar male voice drawled behind her. Michelle twisted in her chair, frowning at the heavyset, dark-haired man who stood behind her. He wore a baggy cotton shirt with horizontal black stripes, pleated cotton slacks and leather thongs. His deep-set eyes were dark, moist and busy, running the length and breadth and width of her. Not slick enough to be a lawyer, Michelle thought. Far too old to be a college student, and too relaxed to be an escaped husband out for a weekend fling. She couldn't peg him, which made her wary.

"I don't think that's any of your business, pumpkin," she replied sweetly.

He laughed, patting her on the head with a heavy hand. "I knew you were different the minute I set eyes on you. How about letting me buy you a drink at the bar?"

"No."

Pat, pat, pat. "One little drink, angel."

His cologne was unmistakable—*Eau de Jack Daniels*. Michelle drew back as far as the table would allow, throwing Thomas Alexander Murphy a speaking look. "Thomas?"

He leaned forward with an inquiring smile. "Yes, sugar lips?"

"Are you enjoying yourself?" she asked politely, ducking that sledgehammer touch.

While Thomas gave serious consideration to her question, the dark-haired man gave her shoulder a hearty squeeze. "The question is whether or not you're enjoying yourself, honey child. I have a feeling you don't know what a good time is."

"Maybe not," she replied, planting the heel of her shoe on his bare toes with some force. "But somehow I don't think it includes having a repulsive alien life-form invade my face."

He grinned, bright-eyed drunk and completely undeterred. "I like a sense of humor. I like funny girls. We could have a terrific time together, you and me."

"Thomas?"

"Right here, honey child," he said promptly. "What can I do for you?"

Michelle glowered at him, peeling a sticky hand off her shoulder. "Nothing at all. I just wanted to include you in the conversation. I didn't want you to feel left out."

"That's sweet."

"Unless you'd like to help me out with my little problem here?"

"Oh. I'm sorry. You're such a spunky little thing, I thought I'd let you take care of it. Oh, well." He sighed and slowly got to his feet, wincing when he realized the love-struck drunk topped him by at least three inches. "Tell me, buddy... are you going to be a nice guy and leave the lady alone?"

"Go to hell, *buddy*."

Thomas looked disappointed. "I didn't think so."

Michelle wasn't sure just what happened next. Either the drunk went for Thomas or Thomas went for the drunk, but the little scuffle was over before most people in the restaurant knew it had even occurred. Thomas stood behind the taller man, twisting the fellow's arm against his back like a pretzel.

"We'll just walk outside now," Thomas said conversationally. "Just the two of us. Is that all right with you?" The man made a sound like a clogged garbage disposal and Thomas nodded at Michelle. "You see? He's very cooperative. I'll just send him on his way and be right back. Oh, here comes Harry wielding a silver tray. Tell him everything's under control."

Michelle watched the pair shuffle awkwardly out of the room, assuring the concerned waiter that Thomas had everything under control. And she believed it, for the first couple of minutes. When Thomas still hadn't returned to the restaurant nearly ten minutes later, she started biting her nails, staring hard at the front doors.

Something had gone wrong.

Thomas wasn't sure where he had gone wrong. Probably he hadn't taken the drunk seriously enough, assuming anyone with that much liquor in him would have the coordination of a dim-witted turtle. Thomas had eased his grip just long enough to flag down a cab, then received a meaty fist in his face for his efforts. The punch was sloppy but surprisingly painful. Thomas had quickly subdued the man

with a powerful left hook, but his pride—and his left eye—
were both killing him.

He bundled the babbling drunk into a passing police
cruiser, declining to press charges. It wasn't the first time
he'd been called on to escort an undesirable element from
Shenanigans, but it was the first time the undesirable element had landed a punch. Thomas wondered if he was getting old, or stupid or both.

He wasn't looking forward to going back into Shenanigans. His sight field was rapidly diminishing, and he could
imagine what his swelling eye looked like. This wasn't supposed to happen to the good guy.

He combed his hair with his fingers, tucked in his shirt
and walked back into the restaurant with his hand partially
obscuring his eye in the most casual way. It didn't work. The
damsel who used to be in distress intercepted him in the
lobby.

"He hurt you!" She gasped, slapping her hands on her
cheeks and staring at him with Tweetybird eyes.

He scowled. "Keep it down, will you, Fats?"

"He *hurt* you," she repeated angrily, looking at the door
as if she would charge on out there and give the fellow a
dose of his own medicine. Then as an afterthought, "And
my name is Michelle."

Michelle. Such a sweet name, Thomas thought. A name
that belonged to a delicate young thing who wore lacy white
collars and didn't know a cue stick from a pogo stick. "The
name doesn't fit you at all," he said, brushing past her. "I'll
call you Mick."

She followed him through a maze of tables. "Where are
you going? You should put some ice on that eye."

"I'm going to my office to put some ice on my eye."

"You have an office here?"

"Yes."

"Why?"

"I own Shenanigans, that's why. And I want to make something perfectly clear to you." He stopped in his tracks, capturing her shoulders in both his hands. He saw her through a fuzzy, one-eyed tunnel. "I'm a victim of my own stupidity, nothing more. I let my guard down for a second and that loudmouthed drunk took me by surprise. It's never happened before and it sure as hell won't happen again. You need to understand that."

"I do?" Curiosity sparkled in her dark eyes. "Why?"

Thomas stared at her intently, brows drawn together, the skin around his injured eye crinkling like dried mud. "I don't know why. It has something to do with wounded pride and pink leather skirts and peanuts. You figure it out, Mick. I'll be back in a few minutes. Don't go away."

His office was located down the hall from the kitchen, a windowless, oak-paneled room cluttered with Thomas's treasures: a fifty-gallon saltwater aquarium that housed a prized collection of tropical fish; a thriving, six-foot potted palm; a giant stuffed marlin mounted on the wall behind his desk; and a life-size cutout of Muhammad Ali delivering a deadly right cross to Joe Frazier. Tonight Thomas felt especially sympathetic toward Smokin' Joe. He took a couple of ice cubes out of a mini-refrigerator and put them in a damp cloth, then held it gingerly over his injured eye. It was swollen completely closed now, and his depth perception was off. He cracked his shin on the leg of the coffee table when he sat down on the couch, which didn't improve his mood any. He sat very still until the throbbing in his leg eased and the right side of his face was numb.

A sad night for white knights, he thought, and his lips twitched in the beginning of a smile. In the past sixty minutes, he'd lost five million dollars, the use of his left eye and any delusions he might have had about his lightning-swift reflexes. A melancholy end for the Golden Gloves Junior Boxing Champion of 1970.

He threw the ice pack down on the table, tipped his head back against the sofa and stared at the ceiling. His smile grew into a lopsided grin. At least he hadn't fallen asleep in his ginger ale tonight. That was the trouble with being a reformed hell-raiser. All too often he found himself wrestling with boredom, that hobgoblin of the respectable life. Thomas was always on the lookout for interesting diversions, and tonight had been one interesting diversion after another. A beautiful blonde. Peanut juggling. A five-million-dollar pool game. A fist fight. All in all, a hell of an entertaining night.

He had no idea what was so funny, but the laughter came anyway, his chest rumbling and jouncing, his eye throbbing. In the middle of it all, he heard a knock at the door. Before he could control the laughter long enough to respond, the door opened in hesitant slow motion.

"Thomas? You all right?" Harry peered cautiously around the door. "I heard noises...like you were in pain, or something."

"I am in pain," he said, when he could. "My ego. My checkbook. My eye. Don't ask me why I'm laughing, I don't know."

"Neither do I," Harry said with great feeling, staring at Thomas's swollen eye. "Well, at least you can breathe easy now. Hurricane Blondie is gone."

A guaranteed smile killer. "She's gone?"

"Yeah. Some guy...Sam, I think she called him—picked her up a few minutes ago. Oh, she left you a message." He pulled a crumpled napkin out of his shirt pocket and handed it to Thomas. "I gotta run. A couple dozen Shriners just showed up and they're moving all the tables around so they can sit together. And they're singing," he added, grimacing. "Man, if I had to wear those silly hats, I sure as hell wouldn't be singing about it. Catch you later."

Harry forgot to close the door when he left and Thomas could hear the Shriners singing. He got up, shut the door, then stood in the middle of the room staring at nothing.

Sam. Thomas had had a gerbil once named Sam. A smelly, mean-tempered little beast. The name alone was enough to make him feel antagonistic.

He read the message scrawled on the napkin.

A black eye is worth more than five million dollars. Consider your debt paid in full. Thanks for everything. Mick.

So much for interesting diversions. Thomas wadded up the napkin and tossed it in the wastebasket. He looked at his watch. It was half past twelve, almost time to close up. There were things to be done, receipts to be totaled, the night deposit to be made. Tedious distractions to fill his mind while he adjusted to the strange blankness he felt. He couldn't for the life of him remember why he had been so happy only a few minutes before.

He worked for several minutes at his desk before his truant thoughts wandered back to her. He remembered the way her diamond earrings caught the light whenever she turned her head, sparkling through the long ivory strands of her hair. He saw her reaching across the pool table for a difficult shot, the pink leather skirt stretching in a dozen breathtaking ways. There was something about smooth, soft, pink things that played merry hell with his concentration.

He swiveled in his leather chair, staring fixedly out the window at the blinking red lights of a tow truck. The last thing he had expected was for her to disappear without a word. Then again, she had yet to do what he expected. He liked that. Reformed hell-raisers loved surprise.

She was ten years younger than he was. He didn't like that. Still, she was experienced enough to have acquired that intimidating ''when hell freezes over'' look of hers. That was intriguing.

She smiled with her eyes. He liked that.

She was a better pool player than Thomas was. He didn't like that.

He dropped his head against the back of his chair and closed his eyes. None of it really mattered. Unless her car broke down again in front of Shenanigans, he doubted he would ever...

A tow truck. Of course.

He was up and out of his chair in a heartbeat, grabbing a pen from his desk. He threw open the office door, shouldering his way through the well-oiled Shriners who stood in line in front of the rest room. He ran through the restaurant and out into the street just as the tow truck pulled away from the curb, a shiny white Mazda RX-7 rolling behind. Thomas stood in the dusty light of a street lamp and scribbled the Mazda's license plate number on the palm of his hand.

''We're going to have so much fun,'' he said, a slow smile teasing the corners of his silver-blue eyes. And then he leaned his shoulder against the lamppost and began to laugh.

Two

Her name was Michelle DeMara. She was indeed twenty-four years old. Her birthday was on December twenty-fifth. Her address was 1612 Cliff Road. She was single, she weighed one hundred and seven pounds and she didn't wear glasses.

Thomas had a friend on the Newport police force. He was willing to provide Thomas with the information from Michelle's driver's license and car registration, as long as Thomas agreed to keep his source confidential...and to tear up his sizable bar tab at Shenanigans.

Three days after the five-million-dollar pool game, Thomas cleaned the empty cola cans out of his car and went for a ride. Like all residents of Newport, he was familiar with the breathtaking Georgian mansions located on Cliff Road. Mini-palaces all, presiding over the rocky coast of the Atlantic Ocean in summer-white splendor. Thomas also knew the ultra-wealthy dominated only a small section of Cliff Road, perhaps three or four miles. On either side they were flanked by the moderately wealthy, and they by the comfortable middle class. For some reason, he expected to find the savvy blond pool player with the smiling eyes living in a modest summer cottage with a colorful flower garden out front.

Expected. That should have been his first warning.

At 4:50 p.m. Thomas parked his 1969 Corvette in front of 1612 Cliff Road. At least he thought it was 1612. There was a football field of velvet lawn between the street and the house, and it was too far away to read the numbers. He counted four levels of windows, sixteen pillars and nine chimneys . . . and that was only from the front.

Fast on the heels of surprise number one came surprise number two. Sixteen-Twelve Cliff Road was hosting a party this afternoon. A huge yellow-and-white striped tent that could have housed the Ringling Brothers Circus billowed in the sea breeze on the south lawn. Doors, windows and lampposts were adorned with white satin ribbon and masses of fresh flowers. White wrought-iron security gates were swung wide, and a glossy parade of Porsches, Mercedeses and limousines were rolling down the red brick driveway at a steady clip.

"I don't think I'm in Kansas anymore," Thomas muttered blankly. He was lost. Michelle DeMara lived here? Mick, with the tight leather skirt and the triple-pierced ears? These people weren't the sort to juggle peanuts. None of it made any sense.

Surprise number three. This wasn't just another tea party for the Junior League, Thomas realized. There were hundreds of guests, the men in tuxedos, the women in extravagant hats and flowing pastel dresses. Uniformed waiters and waitress worked the crowds like busy little ants, silver trays flashing. High on the terrace above the lawn was seated what appeared to be an entire symphonic orchestra.

This was a wedding. Someone at 1612 Cliff Road was getting married today.

Thomas liked interesting diversions. He hated nasty surprises.

Michelle wasn't looking forward to walking down the aisle. Her skirt was a little too long, and she kept catching the heel of her shoe on the hem. Besides, there was something about having five hundred pairs of eyes focused on you that kind of took the spring out of your step. She would be enormously relieved when the whole thing was over.

Her father poked his head in the door, dark eyes sparkling above ruddy cheeks. "Darling Mick, I've never seen you look more beautiful."

Michelle dropped the choker of pearls she was trying to fasten around her neck. "You haven't called me Mick since I was twelve."

"Angel girl, on a day like today, a man feels nostalgic. I'm so proud of my beautiful daughter, I could burst. Here, let me help you." He picked up the necklace, working the clasp with clammy fingers. "Damn thing's stuck. Hold still...there we go, all right and tight."

Michelle wet her dry lips with the tip of her tongue. "What time is it?"

"Almost six," Patrick DeMara replied, kissing his daughter on both cheeks. "Give your dad a little smile. It's going to be a grand affair, love. Well, then...are we ready?"

Michelle managed a tiny smile. "Just about. I'll be downstairs in a minute, Dad."

"Not too long, Mick. The guests are waiting." Patrick left the room, whistling "Get me to the Church on Time." Michelle sat down heavily on the edge of the bed, her hands folded tightly in her lap. She could hear violins through the open window, the gentle murmur of voices. Another thirty minutes and it would all be over. Another thirty minutes and her entire life would be changed. Again.

"I don't simper, cringe or hesitate," she said aloud. "Also I have an interesting attitude and I can juggle peanuts. I can make it through one simple wedding."

A little pep talk, courtesy of Murphy Babe. She hadn't thought of him much in the past few days. She hadn't had time to think. But now she found the memory of his smile and his teasing comments strangely comforting.

She stood with a sigh, smoothing the crushed skirt of her gown. It was time.

Thomas was wearing white sneakers, beige cotton slacks and a dark blue shirt. Fortunately he'd unearthed a wrinkled tie in the trunk of his car. The usher who greeted him at the tent looked a little startled, but managed a polite smile. "Friend of the bride or groom?" he asked.

Thomas considered. If Mick was getting married today, she was no friend of his. Still, he would think positively. "The bride," he said.

He was seated next to a wide-bodied matron in a floppy-brimmed straw hat that scratched him in the ear whenever she turned her head. She started talking in a stage whisper the moment he sat down.

"Hardly a match made in heaven, is it?" she said.

Thomas looked at her, ducking the bobbing hat. "Isn't it?"

"These May-December things never work out. Besides, he's been a widower for less than a year. I can't feel good about it."

Thomas nodded, making no attempt to speak. He wasn't sure he could.

"Oh, he's terribly charming," the woman went on, tossing her hands into the air. "Why, I went to lunch with him once or twice myself, and...well, that's neither here nor there. He's too old for her. I don't care how charming he is, you can't ignore the difference in their ages."

Thomas stared at her with a lowering brow. "I can't say I know the groom all that well. Just how old would you say he is?"

"My goodness. He's closer to sixty than fifty. You tell me what on earth they could possibly have in common."

The wedding march began. Eyes wide and growing wider, Thomas watched as a distinguished, silver-haired gentleman took his place at the altar. His cheeks were flushed, his eyes sparkled with anticipation and his beaming smile included one and all in his happiness. Thomas slumped down in his seat and dropped his chin against his chest. "Maybe he plays pool," he said dully.

"What's that?"

"Nothing. Never mind." Thomas's emotions were playing leapfrog with one another in a nauseating fashion. Damn all interesting diversions from this day forward. He was cured forever.

He had a sudden memory of Mick's dark brown eyes, so filled with personality and humor. He was stupefied. An irrational, overwhelming sense of loss grew up around him like a thundercloud. He wanted to kick something.

"The daughter's quite pretty," the woman beside him remarked in a condescending tone. "A little flashy for my taste, though."

After a moment, Thomas opened his good eye, hardly daring to hope. "Daughter? Whose daughter?"

"The groom's daughter. Michelle." A thoughtful pause here. "The hair can't be natural, not with that stunning color. Still, she makes a nice bridesmaid."

The groom's *daughter*.

Thomas let out a breath he hadn't been aware of holding. He turned his head slowly, feeling the soft brush of air against his face as Michelle DeMara proceeded down the aisle with a slow, measured step. He didn't see who came before her, or who came behind. Her shoulders were bare above the pale yellow gown she wore, and he could see the creamy white curve that began her breasts. Her small, boy-ish hands were lost in a lush bouquet of white and yellow roses. A glossy mother-of-pearl comb held her hair high on her head, a few pale strands working loose and collapsing on the back of her neck.

And pearls. She wore a lustrous pearl choker at her throat and three perfect pearls in her triple-pierced ears. For the first time since arriving at 1612 Cliff Road, Thomas smiled. He very much doubted there was another woman within a three-mile radius who had triple-pierced ears.

"Hey, Mick," he whispered softly.

Michelle stumbled, completely losing the rhythm of the music. Her head swiveled; her startled gaze found Thomas Murphy in a sea of nameless faces. His blue eyes seemed unnaturally bright in the shadows of the tent, and there was something in his smile that made her heart slam against her ribs.

"She doesn't have much rhythm." The woman next to Thomas sniffed.

"She's got great eye-hand coordination, though," Thomas murmured.

"It's a simple step and slide," the woman whispered.

"And she's a hell of a pool player," Thomas added, never taking his eyes from Michelle's face. His smile stretched slowly, both tender and teasing and meant only for her.

Michelle's thoughts were a quagmire, a cloud of pink color spreading over her cheeks. She wasn't aware she had stopped dead in the aisle until the bridesmaid waiting behind her gave a pointed nudge with the toe of her shoe. She started walking again, counting to herself, trying and failing to find the proper pace. She would think about Thomas Murphy later, try to understand why on earth he was sitting here at her father's wedding. Later.

"Marriage is a hallowed institution, ordained in the eyes of God. It is a union of souls, where two become one. Take strength from each other, live joyfully together in this uncertain world . . ."

She looked at Thomas only once during the ceremony. Tawny in the hazy light that filtered through the silk tent, his expression composed to near solemnity, he winked at her with a rainbow-colored eye.

Three

―――

He wanted to take her to a tropical island with soft breezes and warm blue water and keep her there forever. They would wear fig leaves—sometimes—and live on love and coconuts.

Thomas had a thing about tropical islands. He thought they were sexy and peaceful, a rare and wondrous combination. He fully intended on buying one someday—or at least a small piece of one—and living out the rest of his days in paradise, playing the harmonica and letting his hair grow and turning as brown and leathery as an old sea turtle. He thought Michelle would fit in his tropical utopia very nicely. She could clap when he played his harmonica. She could weave flower crowns for her glorious blond hair. Of course, she would wear sunscreen when they frolicked naked on the beach, because she wouldn't want to become leathery like Thomas.

In your dreams, Murphy.

Thomas stood with his shoulder propped against a white marble pillar, watching Michelle as she began yet another dance with yet another partner. She seemed perfectly at home among the primped and pampered, a far cry from a wild island wench. Still, he could fantasize. She would be such a sweet addition to Murphy's paradise.

The setting sun bathed the dancers on the flagstone terrace in a warm, honeyed light, making every movement look enchanted, effortless. Thomas knew this to be a sad illusion as far as he was concerned. He'd never leaned to dance in his younger years, at least, he'd never learned to enjoy dancing. Oh, he had been famous for his fancy footwork in a boxing ring, but put him on a dance floor and the magic died. He was older and more sophisticated now, but no more comfortable with the dreaded box step than he'd been at eighteen. Consequently he'd spent the past forty-five minutes catching brief glimpses of Michelle's dark-lashed gaze over the shoulders of other men. Cutting in on her would be cruel; she was wearing fragile, open-toed sandals that would provide little protection against his unnatural rhythm. And so he watched and waited, just as he'd done since the wedding party had migrated to the flagstone patio bordering the olympic-size pool. Several times following the ceremony, Michelle had started toward him, questions in her wide brown eyes, but inevitably someone had intercepted her. This sort of thing was not going to be a problem in Murphy's paradise. There would be no dancing allowed on his island, with the exception of the occasional hula set to harmonica music.

If he were a gentleman, Thomas thought, he'd leave the lady to play hostess and come back at a more convenient time. Then again, if he were a gentleman, he probably wouldn't have crashed the party in the first place. He followed the elegant swirl of pale silk as Michelle brushed past him in a graceful turn of the dance. The waning light spilled over her bare shoulders, casting warm, golden shadows on the delicate rise of her breasts. Her eyes were very dark, unreadable, sparkling with hectic color. Her smile was brilliant, directed at her partner, the company at large, everyone and no one at all. She looked exquisite, self-possessed...and somehow fragile.

Sweet Michelle, what a picture you make. Methinks you would do wonderful things for fig leaves.

Thomas sighed, his own eyes tucked at the corners with a reluctant smile. Ah, well. Desperate situations called for desperate measures. He would dance.

He fortified himself with a glass of champagne before making his daring move. Michelle was dancing with a young Fred Astaire who shuffled, dipped and twirled with frightening enthusiasm. Thomas had to circle him twice before he managed to get close enough to tap him on the shoulder.

"I'm sure you don't mind," Thomas said, taking Michelle into his arms with all the finesse of an accomplished dancer. "Old friend of the family, you know."

Fred's sparkling grin faltered. "Well, I suppose...if Michelle wants..."

"Does Michelle want?" Thomas asked softly, holding her in an inquiring gaze. Michelle's eyes focused with new awareness, her smile softening into something less brilliant but more sincere. He felt that childlike smile in every bone and sinew of his body.

"Yes," she said simply.

I'm in trouble, he thought, grinning inwardly. Sweet, deep trouble, which is exactly what I came for.

Thirty seconds into the dance, Michelle guessed his secret.

"You hate this," she said. "You hate dancing."

Thomas shook his head emphatically. "Lady, I live to dance. Mind your foot. Damn, I'll bet that hurt." This as he grazed her bare toes with his shoe. "Sorry. I'll be more careful."

"Thomas, what are you doing here?"

"Right now I'm counting."

Michelle's eyes sparkled as she noticed his lips moving almost imperceptibly. The man was indeed counting, his brow furrowed in earnest, endearing concentration. He gave no sign of being aware of the curious glances he drew from the wedding guests. Thomas Alexander Murphy had no interest in "making an impression," which in itself guaranteed him a fair amount of attention. She tried to make an objective inventory of him, this man with the careless mane of honey-brown hair and the lively, demon-bright eyes. The lean, fluent lines of his body, dressed in simple cotton slacks and a loose navy shirt, made every other man at the party seem overdressed. His dancing left something to be desired, yet she very much doubted that fact kept him awake at night. With Thomas Murphy, what you saw was what you got. No apologies made, no disguises and no defenses. She wondered how he managed it. She wondered how anyone managed it in this world.

"Would you like a glass of champagne?" Thomas asked, noticing she had lost her smile. He supposed dancing with him was more of a strain than he realized. "We could sit down and talk for a minute...unless you need to see to your guests?"

"Technically they're not my guests," she said. "They're my father's. And I'd love some champagne, thank you." She'd already had two glasses of the bubbly, but her party spirit remained stubbornly flat.

They sat on the low edge of a stone wall that surrounded the patio. There were roses and fuchsias planted nearby, and Michelle could smell their rich fragrance above the aroma of champagne and food. She sipped her drink, watching her father dance with his blushing new bride. She'd never seen him look happier...at least, not since his last wedding. And as for Michelle's brand-new stepmama, only ten years older than Michelle herself...well, who knew what the future would bring? Sophie Quinn DeMara was a nice enough woman, an economics professor, no less. Her light brown hair was naturally curly, with a tendency to wander, and her wide-set gray eyes only occasionally gave way to merriment. In a crowd, heads would never turn to look at her, but Patrick DeMara was obviously smitten.

"They both look very happy," Thomas commented, following the direction of Michelle's gaze.

Michelle nodded, her feet swinging idly beneath the hem of her gown. "There's nothing my father enjoys more than a wedding. When he and Virginia were married, they had an incredible firework display at the reception. And pigeons."

Thomas set his drink carefully on the stone wall, then gave his full attention to Michelle. "Virginia? Pigeons?"

"No, not really pigeons," Michelle corrected herself, frowning. "Doves. At least, I think they were doves. Anyway, they were released at sunset just before the fireworks. I swear, there were hundreds and hundreds of them, and I have no idea where they all flew off to. Lord help us if they ever come back. Virginia was my father's third wife," she added almost incidentally.

After a pause, "Third wife?"

"Virginia Adelson. She owned—" Michelle indicated the house and grounds with a sweep of her hand "—all this, plus a nifty share of Rhode Island. She was a few years older than my father, but they seemed happy enough. They were married barely a year before she died of a stroke."

"I'm sorry." It was the only thing vaguely appropriate Thomas could think of to say. Doves and fireworks, third marriages, fourth marriages . . . and Michelle's husky voice reciting it all with gentle detachment. He could hardly take it in.

"Things happen," Michelle replied softly, expressionlessly. "I really didn't know Virginia very well. While they were married, she and Daddy spent all their time traveling." Monte Carlo, Atlantic City, Vegas . . . and an unlimited bankroll. Paradise on earth for Patrick DeMara.

"Anyway, she'd been married once before, but there were no children, so...she divided her entire fortune between Daddy and her favorite charity. Kind of a fifty-fifty split."

His gaze never left her face. The warm colors of the dying day accented the stark simplicity of Michelle's expression. Her thoughts were her own, her dark eyes gave away nothing. The lady was a blank page when she wanted to be.

Things happen, she'd said. Thomas was no stranger to the harsh realities of life, but he experienced an unfamiliar tightness in his chest when he looked at the perfectly composed young woman beside him. At the tender age of twenty-four, Michelle was already a survivor. He felt pity, which he knew she wouldn't appreciate, and a sudden need to touch her, which she probably wouldn't appreciate, either.

He clasped his hands in his lap to keep them from straying. "So you weren't born a member of the privileged class?"

"Are you kidding?" She chuckled softly. "I was born a member of the huddled masses. I still bite my fingernails and I buy clothes straight off the rack. I chew gum and I never know which fork to use at a formal dinner and I buy my panty hose in plastic eggs at the grocery store. I'm a dismal failure as Cinderella, believe me. No matter what I wear, no matter what I do or say, I still feel like I've got soot all over my face."

Thomas tipped his head, studying her with a quizzical half smile. Then he lifted his hand, slowly tracing the warm curve of her cheekbone with his index finger. "No soot," he said softly, holding up his hand for inspection.

His voice was gentle. His eyes crinkled endearingly at the corners in that way he had, boyish and almost innocent. Almost...but not quite. Longing washed through Michelle unexpectedly, a fierce desire to be taken into his arms and...

And hugged, she thought wistfully. Hugged, like a sleepy baby at naptime, a frightened child, or just a cherished friend. Still lost in those come-hither eyes, she absently raised her glass, draining the last of her champagne. Thomas Alexander Murphy was very comfortable to be with, she decided almost sadly. Just the sort of man she wished would give her a warm, comforting hug about now.

And she was getting incredibly morbid. She broke away from the warm sensuality in his gaze and stared down at her empty glass with a frown. Three or four drinks and suddenly she was dog-paddling in self-pity. She'd never had a taste for alcohol, but she'd always assumed the more you drank, the better you felt.

"I should have known," she murmured. Of course Michelle DeMara would be an exception to the rule. She always was.

Thomas lifted her chin in the crook of his finger. "What?"

"I said I should go," she replied, deliberately pulling back from his compelling touch. She stood, making a great production of smoothing her wrinkled skirts. Gloom. Depression. Melancholy. They crowded her, making her throat burn and her chest ache. It was time to stop thinking. It was probably time to stop drinking, as well. "I saw my father wave to me— I think Sophie is getting ready to throw her bouquet. They have a plane to catch in a couple of hours. They're going to Nice for their honeymoon."

Thomas pushed himself slowly off the wall, regarding her steadily. Abracadabra, Michelle was back in her pretty little shell. One moment he sensed a bond between them, hovering and uncertain; the next, they were polite strangers who had shared nothing more than a drink. And he could tell by the set of her lips and the studied tone of her voice that she wanted it that way. He wondered if she realized how much more she revealed by her sudden withdrawal. Obviously pity frightened her. She hadn't much experience with friendship, and less with trust.

This was going to take some time.

"I don't bite," he said mildly.

Michelle looked startled, then a wry smile touched her lips. "Everybody bites, Thomas Murphy. It amazes me that you could have reached the ripe old age of . . ." She paused, raising an inquiring brow. "Just how old are you?"

He gave her his most winsome smile. "Old enough to know better," he said, "for all the good it does me. Enjoy the ball, Cinderella. I shouldn't monopolize your time, considering I wasn't invited in the first place."

"Wait a second—that reminds me. You never explained why you were here. How did you find my house? How did you find out my name? Who told you—"

"So many questions, and so little time." Thomas sighed. "I'll explain everything later. In the meantime, I want you to have this." He reached into his hip pocket and pulled out a rather crumpled check. "Here. My first monthly install-ment payment."

Completely bewildered, Michelle took the check. "What is this? Twelve dollars and fifty cents?"

"We had an honest wager," he replied solemnly. "I al-ways honor my debts, Mick. I figure at this rate, I should have you paid in full in about thirty-three thousand years, give or take a few hundred."

"You tracked me down to give me twelve dollars and fifty cents?"

"You're missing the big picture, Mick. I tracked you down to pay you five million dollars. Gradually." Smile lines deepened around his wide mouth. "Looks like this is the beginning of a long, long friendship, wouldn't you say?"

Michelle looked from Thomas to the check in her hand. "This is ridiculous. You don't owe me anything. I told you last week when that obnoxious drunk beat you up—"

"Took me by surprise."

Michelle nodded impatiently. "All right. Took you by surprise. But the fact is, if it hadn't been for me, you wouldn't be sporting that shiner. That makes us even."

"Not in my book." Thomas pushed his hands deep in his pockets, rocking back and forth on the balls of his feet. "It's a debt of honor, ma'am. Whether it's five million or five hundred, the principle is the same. I couldn't live with myself if I didn't make every effort to meet my obligation. As a matter of fact, if you'd like to have an attorney draw up some sort of legal—'

"Enough already!" Dark eyes flashing with exasperation, she stuffed the check in the ruffled bodice of her dress. "I'll take your twelve dollars and fifty cents every single month for the next thirty-three thousand years. Your principles are intact."

"I never said that." His amused gaze was riveted on her low-cut neckline. "Do you know, I just remembered a bit of spare change I meant to give you, too. Yes, a few quarters, a couple of dollar bills...do you think you have room there?"

"Very funny." Out of the corner of her eye, Michelle caught her father's impatient look. She nodded and waved at him. "I need to go, Thomas. They're all waiting for me."

"Are you going to be all right?" Idiot. Of course she was going to be all right. This was her home, these were her friends. He was the intruder in this glossy scenario. Still, her eyes sparkled with a hectic brightness that reminded him of something close to panic. Or tears. He would have liked to pull her close and just...comfort her. But Thomas Murphy knew himself fairly well, and he figured his brotherly compassion would last about three seconds once he had her in his arms. His libido wasn't quite as reformed as the rest of him.

His words brought her chin up sharply, which hardly surprised him. Mick didn't appreciate sympathy. "Why would you say that?" she asked tersely.

"Forgive me, I lost my head. Go back to your guests, Cinderella. You can dance for hours yet, midnight's a long way off."

Too far off. She brushed back a wisp of her hair distractedly. "What about you? Are you going to be—" She paused, clamping her lips shut. Of course he was going to be all right. He found his way in, he could find his way out. "Well, then . . . I'll say good-night."

His mouth tugged up at the corners. "Well, then . . . I'll say good-night, too."

Michelle took a deep breath, turned on her heel and walked across the terrace toward her father and Sophie. Immediately she was swallowed up in people—kiss-kiss, lovely party, must get together, darling. Perfect teeth, exotic perfumes, glittering jewels, exaggerated compliments . . . *gloom.*

Michelle's father and her new stepmother left for the airport at 10:30 p.m. The last of the wedding guests finally wandered off around midnight, and the caterers left not long after that. Michelle was exhausted. The only live-in help consisted of the housekeeper, Mrs. Bruderer, and her husband, Milo, a jack-of-all-trades who served as butler, handyman and chauffeur. Michelle sent them off to their quarters in the gate house, with instructions to take a long weekend. They had both worked above and beyond the call of duty preparing for the wedding reception.

Which left Cinderella alone in the castle with her aching feet and a ferocious, woman-eating depression.

She should have refused the last two glasses of champagne toward the end of the evening, but the guests persisted in making toast after toast to her father and Sophie, and she didn't want to appear petty or ungracious. A fourth wedding could be a little tricky, and she didn't want to give the gossips any more ammunition than they already had. By the time the reception ended, the unaccustomed amounts of alcohol had reduced her to one of the most pathetic and sorrowful creatures on the face of the earth.

Lips quivering, eyes misting, she started up the wide circular staircase that led to the second, third and fourth levels of the house. Her bedroom was on the third floor, miles and miles and miles away. She stopped on the second step to take off her shoes. She stopped on the fourth step to sit and rest, and to try and decide if she would rather sleep on the oriental carpet in the foyer than walk the rest of the way to her room.

The house was completely dark. It was a fitting place to sniffle and brood, sitting there on the stairs in a deserted mansion where she could be alone with the blue devils. She muttered a few descriptive words, unusual expletives picked up in pool halls and gambling dens in her younger years. She tossed her shoes at the front door, but her aim was off and she hit the potted palm instead. She was distressed and amazed at her lack of control, but there seemed nothing she could do to stem the glutted spill of self-pity. Her eyes burned from the effort of holding back her tears. She wouldn't cry. She *wouldn't*.

Someone knocked on the front door, three heavy raps. Startled, Michelle gasped, choked on the knot in her throat and began to cough.

"Michelle?" The masculine voice was faint but unmistakable. Thomas.

Michelle struggled for air, pounding herself on the chest.

"Mick! Is that you? Are you all right?"

Still coughing, she stumbled to the door, resting her forehead and both palms against the polished oak. "Stop...asking me...if I'm all right." She gasped hoarsely, trying to catch her breath. "I'm always all right!"

"Damn it, open the door."

"Damn it, I'm going—" Her voice broke. "I'm going to bed. Good night."

"Are you crying?"

She couldn't deal with this. She was far too depressed to deal with anything. She turned without another word, starting up the stairs with grim determination. This time she would make it to the third floor or die trying. Thomas Murphy could spend the night on the front porch with the mosquitoes and the fireflies.

She'd forgotten she hadn't locked the door. It didn't take long for Thomas to figure it out, though. She had barely reached the first landing before he strode inside, slamming the door behind him. "Mick? Where are you?"

Michelle stood there on the landing, not knowing what to say or where to go next. Wishing she were invisible. She hiccuped, and he swiveled to face the stairs. Neither of them moved.

A moment of quiet passed before he spoke. "I can't see anything. Where's the light switch?"

Heaven have mercy, not the light. She didn't want him to see her like this, quivering like jelly and fighting a losing battle against the tears. She took a deep breath, her fist on her stomach. "I don't know what you're doing here, but I'm exhausted. I'm going to bed."

He found the light switch all by himself. The crystal chandelier high above the entry hall blazed to life, flooding the stairway with a harsh white light. Thomas's eyes widened as he studied the blond ghost on the first landing, taking in the unnatural pallor of her skin and the misery in her bruised, deep-set eyes. Her hair was collapsing around her shoulders, her bangs were tangled in her eyes and her nose was suspiciously pink.

"And a good time was had by all," he said.

She sank to her knees on the carpet, her hands lost in the silky folds of her dress. Thomas was staring at her like a pool hustler mulling over a particularly difficult shot. Difficult but not impossible. "Why did you come back?" she asked wretchedly.

"Your eyes." His heavy-lidded gaze was uncomfortably thorough. "They gave you away tonight. You weren't happy. I thought maybe you could use a friend."

That unnerved her, the fact she could have been so transparent, but she was not about to let him know how much. "Of course I was happy. I'm still happy. I would be even happier if you went home and left me—"

"Don't," he said softly. "Just . . . don't."

Michelle held his gaze as long as she could, her heartbeat hard and uneven. When her vision blurred with stinging-hot tears, she dropped her head, burying her chin in a cool yellow ruffle. "Turn the lights off, please. It hurts my eyes."

He turned it off. When his eyes became adjusted to the darkness, he walked slowly up the stairs. He didn't ask any questions, although he wanted to. He knew he had already seen too much as far as Michelle was concerned.

Instead he sat down beside her, his legs drawn up, his arms looped over his knees. And waited.

"I wish you'd go home," she whispered.

"I know."

"You keep turning up."

There was a faint smile in his voice. "Bad pennies—and bad boys—do that."

She turned her head to look at him, her eyes a misty sheen in the darkness. "Are you?"

Her voice had a dreamy, wistful huskiness that stirred him. Thoughts he was almost afraid to recognize came and went in his mind like fleeting shadows, emotions that had little to do with sympathy and concern. *Nothing* to do with sympathy and concern, he amended slightly, his gaze drifting to the moist softness of her trembling lips. "Am I what?"

"A bad boy," she whispered.

"I was, once upon a time." Then, his voice dropping to match hers in softness and intensity, "It's a hard habit to break."

He placed his fingers against her mouth, tracing the full, trembling curves with infinite gentleness. Learning her. Wondering what it would be like if he took advantage of her vulnerability and moved closer—like this—and parted her lips with his fingertip, like this....

His mouth came down upon hers slowly, the brush of his lips no heavier than a sigh. Not yet a kiss, but so tantalizing, so tempting, his heart began slamming into his ribs, as if he'd been running hard. He heard the breath catch in her throat, watched her tangled, damp lashes slowly drift closed. And then his eyes closed, too, and the pressure of his lips deepened ever so slightly, beginning a caressing massage. Clinging, breaking, meeting again, a rhythmic, erotic explanation. Only a kiss, yet his skin grew hot and desire spilled into the depths of his body. Only a kiss, yet he couldn't smother the yearning that overwhelmed him. He wanted her then and there, with her tear-damp lashes and her dark, tired eyes and all the confusion and hesitation in the world still between them. His hand was on her waist, moving to cup her breast, when she spoke against his lips in a slurred, husky whisper.

"I don't tolerate it."

His head lifted. "What?"

"Alcohol. I thought if I drank enough, it would make things easier, cheer me up. I tried, but it just didn't work that way." She took a deep, betraying breath that sounded more like a sob. His kiss had moved her to tears ... literally. She didn't know why, but suddenly the level of emotion he had aroused in her was unbearable, shattering in its intensity. The emotion of the past twelve hours was unbearable, the past twelve years ...

The dam finally broke, there on the first floor landing of the dark mansion on Cliff Road. Tears spilled over, making weary, burning tracks on her cheeks and chin. She slashed them away with angry hands, but still they came.

"I'm sorry. Thomas, I'm so sorry. I'm all right, I really am."

"You're always all right." His voice was quite gentle, though his pulse still ran like rain. "I know."

"All that champagne...it didn't make me happier. It didn't help at all." Her breath came fast, between the sobs, in painful catches. "It just made everything more...intense. I'm all right, really. I'm just so...*depressed*. How did things get to be like this?"

"Like what?" He stroked back her bangs, his fingers shaking from the effort of bringing himself under control. All the sadness in the world was reflected in her tear-bright eyes. "Tell me, Mick. What things?"

"Me. My life. How did it get to be like this? My father's flying the friendly skies with his fourth wife and I'm wandering around this mausoleum trying not to break anything valuable." She was babbling. She shut her eyes tight and tried to concentrate. Important things. "I'm twenty-four years old. Do you know what's upstairs in my bedroom?"

He took her cold hands in his, gently uncurling her clenched fingers. "What?"

"A night-light. I swear to heaven. This stupid night-light you plug into the wall. I hide it in my lingerie drawer during the day so the housekeeper doesn't see it." In the back of her mind, she was horrified at her confessions, but she couldn't seem to stop. "I can't sleep without it. When I was little, my father and I traveled around all the time. I had this Mickey Mouse night-light. No matter where we were, no matter what hotel or what city, I always had it with me."

A Mickey Mouse night-light. Thomas smiled and kissed her on the tip of her nose. Poor baby. She was going to hate herself in the morning for letting the—mouse—out of the bag. "Lots of people can't sleep without a light on. You're not so different."

"Not so different?" She gave a watery laugh. "If only you knew. There are so many things..."

"What sort of things?" he asked soothingly. "Tell me."

Michelle stared at him for a very long time, trying to re-member what she had been going to say. It was useless. She was hollow and floating, and the tears had dwindled to an occasional wet sniffle. "I think I should go to sleep now," she said finally, as if it were a difficult decision arrived at after much deliberation.

A suppressed smile twitched at the corners of her lips. "Bright eyes, you should have gone to sleep about four minutes ago. Lord knows, you'll wish you had in the morn-ing. Where's your room?"

Now there was a depressing subject. Michelle sighed, wanting nothing more than to curl up on the stairway and go to sleep. "My room is way, way—" she gestured upward with a limp hand "—way up there. Third floor. End of the hall, the very end."

"Can you make it?" He was already lifting her to her feet, his arm firmly around her waist.

"Of course I can." Somehow her feet got tangled up in her skirt and she stumbled, coming up hard against his chest. He smelled wonderful, he felt rock steady and there was a nice broad shoulder to snuggle up against. Very com-forting, considering that her kneecaps had disappeared. "I'm not incapacitated, I'm just a little—"

"Inebriated," Thomas supplied helpfully. "Right face, Mick, or you'll go headfirst over the railing."

Though she continued to insist in a rather soggy voice that she was perfectly all right, Michelle was grateful for the support of his arm around her shoulders. It was an ex-hausting journey to her bedroom. The darkness was kind to her stinging eyes, but it slowed their progress considerably. They climbed a million stairs, traversed a hundred miles of hallway and negotiated a sitting room the size of Versailles before she finally found her bed. Her wonderful bed.

Her first impulse was to immediately climb beneath the covers and bury her aching head in a pillow. But she had a man in her room, a man who even now supported her limp body in his arms. She cudgeled her weary brain, trying to come up with the proper thing to say. Thank you for a lovely evening? No, no, no. She started to giggle, though she knew perfectly well there was no humor in the situation.

"Don't get hysterical on me," Thomas said.

She stopped giggling. Immediately a fresh batch of tears threatened. "I am not hysterical."

"I know." He shook his head and smiled, his thumb gently caressing the edge of her collarbone. "You're perfectly all right."

"No." She rubbed her cheek against the cool fabric of his shirt, feeling the taut muscles of his chest beneath. His heartbeat synchronized perfectly with the demon throbbing under her scalp. "I have a headache."

"And it's going to get worse before it gets better, brown eyes." Gently he turned her in the circle of his arms, both hands lifting to frame her face. It was too dark to see her expression, but he could feel her exhaustion. He could also smell the elusive fragrance of her musky perfume and see the moist shimmer of her eyes. His throat was suddenly desert dry, and he felt a chill of desire pass like electricity through his veins. He could feel her hips swaying innocently against his thighs, and he burned there. Thomas had a panicked moment while he fought to control the powerful urges within him. After a long hesitation, his hands began moving softly, soothingly, over her hair. When he finally spoke, his tone was light, but not so devoid of feeling as he would have liked. "You should sleep now. You've had a long day. Being perfectly all right all the time can be exhausting."

Her sigh was heartbreaking. "I can't sleep now."

Her hands were clinging to his shoulders, the tips of her breasts brushing softly against his chest. Willpower, Thomas reminded himself, feeling the muscles in his abdomen knot with tension. Whatever his baser instincts were demanding, he knew the timing was all wrong. "Why not?"

"I'm going to be sick," she replied quite clearly.

Thomas might have been new to the principle of selflessness, but he was intimately acquainted with the common hangover. Quickly he set her down on the edge of the bed, then pushed her head between her knees. "There. No, stay down . . . take deep, slow breaths. You're going to be fine."

Crossly, her voice muffled by her skirt, "I'm going to have a stiff neck. I'm not a pretzel, I don't bend like this."

"Breathe, Mick, don't talk. Where do you keep your aspirin?" When she didn't answer, he added sardonically, "You can talk long enough to tell me where the aspirin is, brat."

"Medicine cabinet in the bathroom."

Thomas made his way carefully across the room, dodging the bulky shadows he could see, banging his shins on invisible things that jumped out at him. Once in the bathroom, he felt along the wall until he found the light switch and flicked it on.

Bathroom? he thought, blinking as his eyes adjusted to the sudden blast of light. This was like no other bathroom he had ever seen in his life. It was far bigger than the billiard room at Shenanigans, a mini-palace of hand-painted tiles and gold fixtures and shimmering glass. The circular bathtub was large enough for six people, situated beneath a stained-glass skylight and surrounded by a miniature rain forest. A nice touch, that little green jungle—it reminded him of his someday island. The countertops were covered with pink Italian marble and the ceiling was edged with gold-leafed crown molding. Thomas had once read about a house where miniature heaters had been installed inside the towel rods in the bathrooms. He slipped his hand beneath a white bath towel and felt the metal rod beneath. Hot. He was momentarily distracted with a beguiling fantasy—sweet Michelle fresh from the bath, swathing her naked body in a warm, downy-soft towel. As a matter of fact, his imagination could have a heyday here, dancing from the pool-sized tub to the transparent shower stall to the luxurious white fur rug on the floor. If he let it. Which he wouldn't.

His breath ragged, he pulled open the door of the medicine cabinet and located the aspirin. He opened the bottle, shook out three, then filled a glass he found on the marble counter with cold water. Before leaving the bathroom, he splashed a little cold water on his face, as well. Every little bit helped.

He left the bathroom light on and the door partially open in deference to his aching shins. He could see now that the bedroom was five times as large as the bathroom and just as luxurious. Michelle looked lost on the king-size bed, a slender figure with her face buried in tumbled pillows.

She was also, Thomas realized belatedly, fast asleep. He gazed down at her for the longest time, then gently set the glass of water and the aspirins on the bedside table. She would need them in the morning.

Though she had fallen asleep on top of the bedspread, there was more than enough to fold over and cover her with. Thomas did so, then stepped back, running his hand through his hair and wondering about his reluctance to leave her. It was this damn house, he thought ruefully. It was too big for one exhausted little pool shark. He played that back in his mind and smiled faintly, surprised at the protective tenderness she inspired in him. Strange that after so many years of emotional apathy, he would suddenly become sensitive to the needs of a defensive, prickly woman-child. He'd never been famous for his noble and compassionate nature.

She turned her head and sighed in her sleep. The fragile curve of her cheek was exposed, edged with a tangled cloud of pale hair. He whispered her name once, touched her cheek lightly, then turned and left the bedroom. Self-control was one thing. Masochism was another.

Heavy double doors separated Michelle's bedroom from the sitting room. Thomas closed them, then made it as far as the door to the hallway before he stopped. The night-light.

He went back into the bedroom, trying to be as quiet as possible. Feeling like an intruder, he pulled open the top drawer of her dresser and slipped his hand inside. Silky things, lacy things, ribbons and sweet-smelling sachets... and a tiny plastic night-light. He plugged it into the socket near the doorway, smiling at the tiny circle of pale yellow light. Such a little glow to provide so much security.

"Thomas?" Michelle was sitting up in bed, her heavy-lidded eyes cloudy and bewildered. "Where are you?"

"I'm right here." The neckline of her gown had pulled to one side, exposing the shadowed curve of her breast. Watching her, Thomas's fingers curled into his palm, his nails digging into his skin. "I was just leaving," he whispered. "Go back to sleep."

"Don't go." She settled back into the pillows and closed her eyes, one slender arm thrown above her head. "Don't want to be here alone... too many noises in this house. Did you hear that?"

"Hear what?"

"Thought I heard something..."

"Everything's fine, Mick. Just sleep."

She turned her head restlessly, her face tight against the pillows. "Hate this house. Too many empty rooms..."

He waited motionlessly until the slow cadence of her breathing told him she was asleep once again. He backed out of the room slowly, this time leaving the double doors between them partially open. He flicked on a lamp in the sitting room, his gaze falling on a pink-and-white striped sofa near the fireplace. He didn't have a great deal of experience sleeping on sofas, but it looked comfortable enough.

It was too late to drive home, anyway. The corners of his wide mouth twisted in a slow smile, his eyes bright with a heated longing. Much too late.

Four

———

Michelle prayed for death.

It might have worked, had she been able to get down on her knees and offer a sincere plea to be put out of her misery. But her throbbing head was sensitive to every movement, every breath, and she didn't dare move from her bed.

She forced her eyelids open, a Herculean effort. The morning sun bounced around her room and suddenly attacked her, burning her eyes, stealing her breath, sending a new wave of pain stabbing through her skull. Too bright, too hot, too obscenely cheerful. There were terrible monstrous birds outside her window, screeching and squawking. Why couldn't there have been a nice rainstorm this morning? Why couldn't there have been an eclipse? She needed darkness and silence. She needed to die in peace.

But if she didn't die, she promised herself grimly, she was going to buy a large cat to eat those birds. Several large cats.

She needed aspirin. She was amazed to find three of them on her night table, along with a glass of water. Mrs. Bruderer? No, she'd given her the weekend off. Then who...?

Thomas.

Her memories of the night before were fuzzy and disjointed, but she did recall Thomas paying a midnight visit. She also remembered asking him to go home, for all the good it had done. He'd come in and sat with her on the stairs and they had talked about...something or other. She couldn't quite remember what came immediately after that, which bothered her a little. Oh, yes, there was that hellish climb to the third floor, while she clung to Thomas like a sick little vine. And there was something else, too. She remembered sitting on her bed, staring at Thomas as he stood in the doorway to the sitting room. His silhouette had been motionless, almost rigid, as if he couldn't decide whether to go or to stay.

She couldn't recall *anything* after that, which bothered her a great deal. Hesitantly she lifted a corner of the bedspread that covered her, breathing a sigh of relief to see her yellow dress more or less in place. That was that, then. Thomas had helped her to the room, left her the aspirins in case she needed them and said good-night like a gentleman. She could live with that.

She sat up in bed, ignoring a scream of protest from her head. If she wasn't going to die, then obviously she should try to ease the pain of living. She took all three pills, silently thanking Thomas for his foresight. She swung her feet over the edge of the bed and stood in thick slow motion, carefully holding her head on her shoulders with both hands. It would be a shame to have it fall off while she wobbled to the bathroom.

A long soak in a steaming bath eased the stiffness from her muscles and gave her the will to live again. Afterward she slipped on a warm velour bathrobe and her fuzzy pink booties, feeling so much better that she decided against buying the bird-eating cats. Perhaps she hadn't been suffering so much from a hangover as from simple exhaustion. A little juice and dry toast and she would be her old self again.

As she walked out of the bedroom, she noticed her nightlight plugged into the wall near the door. That was odd. She usually plugged it into the north wall, near the bed. Ah, well, last night she was probably too tired to tell north from west. She pulled it out of the socket and dropped it back into her lingerie drawer. She couldn't help but feel a little self-conscious, even though she knew no one was watching her. Night-lights, like fourth weddings, could be a little tricky... especially when they belonged to a twenty-four-year-old woman.

Michelle's determinedly optimistic attitude took a sudden nose-dive when she walked into the kitchen and discovered a half-naked man rummaging through the refrigerator. She gasped and stopped dead, skidding several inches on the tile floor in her booties. Her sight field was limited to a firmly muscled, sun-browned back and atrociously wrinkled cotton slacks slung low on lean hips. Thomas Alexander Murphy peered around the refrigerator door, his blond-on-brown hair falling about his face. "Hey, Mick. I was just going to come upstairs and check you for a pulse."

"Thomas?" Her voice came out as a throttled, embarrassing squeak. "Omigosh. You?"

"Yes, cupcake," he said with a glimmer of amusement. "Omigosh me." He kicked the refrigerator door shut with his foot, his arms full of eggs, cheese and orange juice. "I'm cooking. I'm used to the kitchen at Shenanigans, so I ought to be able to find my way around this stainless-steel wonderland of yours. How do you feel about a cheese omelet?"

She shook her head mutely, staring with unblinking eyes. In the dusty morning light, his muscled flesh looked almost golden, his abdomen spare and taut. His hips swayed when he walked with the most natural, primitive... Michelle's eyes began to water. She jerked her gaze upward, meeting lazy blue eyes that sparkled with bright innocence. In that second, she had a flash of memory that had nothing whatsoever to do with innocence. Her mind gave her the exquisite pressure of his mouth moving against hers, his fingers spreading through the air, the warmth of his body pressing against hers....

She couldn't prevent the husky little moan of distress that escaped her lips. Her fingers clutched the belt of her robe in a death grip. "I didn't know you were still here," she said hoarsely.

He set his supplies on the work island in the center of the kitchen, frowning over his bare shoulder. "Of course I'm still here. You asked me to stay. Besides, after last night, did you think I'd just take off and leave you?"

Michelle needed to sit down. She walked over to the kitchen table and dropped like a stone into a high-backed Shaker chair. She took a deep, sustaining breath, feeding much-needed oxygen to her sluggish brain. "I asked you to stay? That's odd. I remember asking you to leave."

He started cracking eggs into a stainless-steel bowl. "Look, no matter how fierce and independent you are, no one is immune to a lonely night every now and then. It's no big deal, Mick. Forget about it."

That was the problem. She already had. "I hope I didn't impose on you." Then, apprehensively, "Well?"

Thomas paused, egg in hand. "Well what?"

"Did I impose on you, or... anything?"

His wide mouth twitched in a smile that suggested he might be laughing inside. Carefully he set the egg back in the carton, then propped one elbow on the counter, chin resting on his palm. "I'm hurt," he said reproachfully, holding her eyes. "You don't remember."

Michelle managed a tight little smile. "Why don't you tell me what it is you think I don't remember, and I'll tell you if you're right or not."

He walked slowly around the counter, his light eyes fairly burning with amusement. She was fishing for information, poor baby. "I have a better idea, Mick. Why don't you tell me what you *do* remember, and I'll fill in the blanks."

"I remember...things. Bits and pieces." Michelle needed to stand. She was restless. She couldn't escape the haunting memory of his mouth, his hands, the quiet darkness that had enfolded them in warmth and intimacy...

Get a grip. She stood abruptly, knocking the chair over backward. By the time she had picked it up and pushed it back under the table, the heat building in her face was suffocating. "I may have had too much to drink last night."

His expressive gaze widened in shock. "No...really?"

Michelle whirled on him, her still-damp hair tangling in her eyes and lashes. She had a choice...either run like a frightened mouse, or stand her ground. Being Michelle, she chose to fight. "Look, Murphy *Babe.* I don't like playing stupid cat-and-mouse games. You know damn well what I want to know, so why don't we cut the—"

"Language, cupcake." He cut short her tirade by grabbing the belt on her robe and pulling her to him, none too gently. Smiling, he raised his hand, wiggling the tip of her indignant nose with his finger. "Calm down. I'd be happy to show you what happened last night." He bent his head, touching his lips gently to hers. He kissed her with the delicate, oh-so-patient eroticism of experience, then slowly withdrew. "There you have it, from beginning to end. You can relax now."

"I will not relax!" In the first place, she didn't need his permission to relax. In the second place, she'd just been turned inside out and upside down by a three-second kiss. A fearful, unsettled feeling was growing inside her, a cross between an upset stomach and trembling desire. Too much, too quickly, and none of it under her control. "If you think I'm going to be put off with that meaningless little kiss, you've got another think coming."

It was too much to resist. She looked flustered and angry and utterly feminine with her startled doelike eyes, her tangled hair and the deep slash in the front of her robe exposing her lush woman's curves. And she was completely sober, relieving him of his wearisome guardian-angel duties. "You've got another think coming, yourself," he said sweetly.

Instinct warned her a second too late. She was stepping backward when his hands closed over her shoulders, dragging her into a kiss that was as violent and sudden as a summer rainstorm. Her hands moved to his chest, where she could feel the pulse of his lifeblood pounding, pounding. Her intention to push him away slipped like sand through her fingers. Her fingers spread over his shoulders, her nails curving into his bare skin. His mouth and tongue played over hers, knowing and hungry. Her lips were open and full to him, a knot of pleasurable tension braiding and unbraiding deep in her stomach. She was intensely conscious of the nakedness of her body beneath the robe, could feel the hard points of her nipples rubbing against the plush velour. She wanted to be touched there; she wanted his hands to lift and caress the swollen weight of her breasts. Never, never in her life had she given herself so mindlessly to pure physical sensation. There was no thinking, no apprehension, and it was such a sweet release to rid herself, even for a brief moment, of her doubts and inhibitions. She heard herself murmur his name in a thick, dreamy voice that seemed to come from far, far away. A stranger's voice, a stranger's body, responding to his touch and his warmth with beautiful, astonishing spontaneity.

She caught her lip between her teeth in anguished delight when his searching hands tenderly parted the soft velour material of her robe, completely exposing her breasts. She felt no shyness, only pleasure as the air tingled over her bare skin, warm as sunlight. And then, even more arousing, the feeling of his fingers pressing and kneading her yearning flesh. Instinctively she strained toward him, rubbing herself against his hands. Wanting more. Hunger she had never dreamed of rose like a tide inside of her.

"Please . . ." she whispered helplessly against his mouth. Pleading for . . . something.

He broke from her, his eyes warm and softly unfocused. "Did you say something about—" he paused to take a betraying breath "—a meaningless kiss?"

Her trembling hands pulled the sides of her robe together. Smears of hot-pink emotion colored her high cheekbones, and she could feel them burning. She stepped backward carefully, because her body felt brittle, as if it might split down the middle if she bumped into anything. "This isn't supposed to happen."

His penetrating blue eyes were glittering with sensual heat. "Oh, yes, it is."

"Oh, no, it *isn't*," she muttered, an edge of panic to her voice. "Not with you. Not like this."

She was finally waking up to him. Her beautiful eyes were lavish with emotion: curiosity, apprehension, growing awareness. He liked that. He couldn't remember the last time a relationship with a woman had progressed in emotional stages. Attraction and satisfaction had always come complete in the same tidy little package. But, of late, he'd felt a nagging impatience with the predictability of things. He wanted a challenge. He wanted the physical enjoyment, but he wanted the uncertainty and the risk and the *feeling* as well. He wanted to experience intimacy again, to assure himself he was still capable of it. He noted the unfamiliar heat of excitement in his chest with pleasure. She'd given him that. The feeling was all the more potent for its long absence from his life.

But first things first. She looked a little pale; he wasn't sure she was still breathing. "You should learn to relax, Mick," he said softly. "Enjoy the unexpected adventures life offers you."

"Such as?"

He smiled encouragingly. "Me."

As she looked into his eyes, she saw the unmistakable promise of erotic mysteries unveiled. Oh, yes... Thomas Alexander Murphy obviously had far more answers than Michelle DeMara had questions. With his knowing hands and come-to-me smile, he was no stranger to earthly pleasures. He promised her adventure. She had absolutely no doubt he was capable of delivering on that promise.

She backed away from him, her hands holding her robe closed at the throat. Her eyes were enormous in her flushed face. She couldn't have blinked if she'd tried. "I'm going to get dressed now."

His gaze took on the faintest edge of amusement. "Chicken."

"This won't happen again, Thomas."

"Whatever you say."

Another two steps backward. "I don't want adventure, do you hear me? I can't deal with this."

He blew her a kiss, his expression companionable. "You underestimate yourself. You can deal with anything. Would you like hash browns or bacon with your omelet?"

Her slim shoulders squared. She stared at him for the longest time, eyes narrowed, as if she could figure out a way to make sense of him if she just tried hard enough. Thomas seemed to find her scrutiny highly entertaining; his smile grew to a full-fledged grin.

She was no match for him. Not like this, when her poor skull was coming apart at the seams. She'd never felt less clever, less articulate, less in control, in all her life. It was time to retreat.

"Hash browns," she said miserably, then turned on her fuzzy pink heel and padded away.

While Michelle was dressing Thomas did what he could to civilize himself. He donned the wrinkled shirt he'd brought downstairs with him, tucking it into his equally wrinkled slacks. He would have liked to shower and shave, but right now he imagined his tread on the stairs would be enough to send Michelle flying out the third-story window. She was spooked.

He could understand her startled resistance—he was a little spooked himself. He was alive with anticipation, impatience, stinging desire...emotions that took him completely by surprise with their fresh jewellike clarity. Anything could happen.

He loved it.

He found a terrific little black-and-white apron in the pantry that looked as if it belonged to a French maid. He put it on and set to work fixing the breakfast his little Michelle didn't want.

While he worked, he whistled. While he whistled, he made enthusiastic plans. He was no oversexed, thrill-seeking adolescent. He intended to savor every unexpected twist and turn of this delightful adventure, as patiently and reverently as his impatient and irreverent nature would permit. Michelle was a chameleon, tough and tender, delicate and daring. Night-lights. Fuzzy slippers. Shaky-hot passion. Never what he expected. He thought it could very well take a lifetime to understand and anticipate her. Fortunately he had all the time in the world.

He heard a soft knocking at the back door. Somehow Thomas couldn't believe the good folk of Cliff Road were in the habit of dropping by for a cozy chat around the kitchen table. This wasn't exactly June and Ward Cleaver territory. He anticipated a deliveryman, or perhaps the postman. When he opened the door, he found a cheerful Jesuit priest standing on the back porch.

Well, he *looked* like a Jesuit priest. He was fair-haired, with a fresh tan and the most sincere smile Thomas had seen in all his life. The fact that he wore a sporty cashmere jacket and silk tie contradicted the priest theory, but still the man exuded clean, high spirits and good cheer. It was a little irritating so early in the morning.

"You're probably not with UPS, either, are you?" Thomas said by way of greeting. He couldn't explain it, but he had a nagging foreboding.

"Excuse me?" The fair-haired fellow frowned briefly, then dimpled again and stuck out his hand. "I'm sorry, I don't believe we've met. I'm Sam Hicks, Michelle's fiancé. And you're...?"

Thomas stared.

Sam Hicks tried again, persistently cheerful. "And you are...?"

Going to kill her, Thomas thought. He put out his hand in stiff slow motion, his fingers closing around Sam Hicks's in a vice grip. "Thomas Murphy. How incredibly interesting to meet you."

"I tried the front door," Sam said apologetically, "but there was no answer. I know how Michelle likes to hide away in the kitchen with a cup of hot chocolate in the morning, so I came around the back. Hope you don't mind."

Thomas glanced at the coffee maker perking away and smiled grimly. So she liked hot chocolate in the morning. Just one little surprise after another. "Why would I mind? I'm just a guest here." *Although I would much rather you toddled around to the swimming pool and did a swan dive into the shallow end.*

Sam's sparkling gaze fell on Thomas's French apron and stuck there. "Hot little number you've got on. Don't be offended, but it looks better on Kirsten."

Thomas looked at Sam's aristocratic nose, thinking how much fun he could have with him in a boxing ring. "Kirsten?"

"The maid. She comes in three times a week. And speaking of coming in . . . ?"

Thomas stepped aside, waving him in. "Like I said, I'm only a guest."

"Thanks." Sam wandered through the kitchen, shrugging out of his jacket and laying it over the back of a chair. He was obviously at home. "I suppose you came for the wedding?"

"That's right." Among other things.

"Member of the family?"

"Friend of the family." Let him chew on that one for a while.

But Sam Hicks, it appeared, was not the suspicious type. He picked an apple from the fruit bowl on the kitchen table and bit into it with great relish. "I felt terrible about missing Patrick's wedding. I pulled emergency-room duty at the hospital, and I couldn't get anyone to cover for me. A real challenging night, too—I spent six hours trying to get a marble out of a two-year-old's nose. Is Michelle awake yet?"

A doctor. He hadn't introduced himself as Dr. Sam Hicks, which indicated he wasn't pretentious. A humble, unsuspicious doctor with a good sense of humor and healthy eating habits. Thomas leaned his hip against the kitchen counter, needing the support. "She should be down in a few minutes. She's dressing." He looked at Sam to see how he would take that bit of news, but the man was absorbed in his apple. Either he had the disposition of a saint, or he didn't consider Thomas Murphy a threat. Thomas disliked saints almost as much as he disliked being taken for granted.

"Knowing Michelle, that could take some time," Sam replied with a good-natured shrug. "Most women only have to pick out one pair of earrings; Michelle has to choose three. Pull up a chair, Murphy. Let's get acquainted. Have you known the DeMaras long?''

Thomas poured two cups of coffee and joined Sam at the kitchen table. His jaw was aching, and he had to consciously force himself to stop grinding his teeth together. "We've had financial dealings," he said.

"Amazing, isn't it, the way Patrick's taken hold of the Adelson Corporation? Michelle expected him to run through it all in a matter of weeks, but he's really calmed down. I'm no expert on compulsive personalities—I specialize in marble extractions—but I think I understand Patrick DeMara. You want to know my theory?''

I'd like to know what the hell you're talking about, Thomas thought. "What's your theory?''

"He's playing the same game he's always played, only with higher stakes. Instead of running down to Atlantic City or Vegas and risking a few thousand dollars, he risks a fortune every day in the stock market. The thrill isn't gone, it's just legitimized. And he's actually doing pretty well at it, from what Michelle tells me. For her sake, I hope he keeps his act together. She's been through enough hell for one lifetime.''

Thomas sat quite still, trying to take it all in. He didn't want to reveal how little he really knew about Michelle. Sam Hicks didn't seem like the kind of person who would pass on gossip simply for the shock value. He thought Thomas was a friend of the family, close enough to be invited to Patrick DeMara's wedding. Obviously he also assumed Thomas knew Michelle's history. "She deserved better," Thomas said slowly. "Although…she seems happier now.''

"Of course she's happier." Sam sat back in his chair, looping his hands behind his neck. "For the first time in her life, she has a permanent home. Can you imagine that poor kid being dragged from town to town, sleeping in rented rooms and pool halls while her dad gambled away every dime they had? And after Michelle's mother got fed up and ran off—how old was Michelle then, six or seven?"

Thomas felt his emotions fading away to a perfect blank. "Something like that."

"Well, then she was gifted with a semienthusiastic string of stepmothers. She once told me she had lived—at least for a night or two—in every state in the continental U.S. She was never in one place long enough to graduate from high school. It's amazing she adjusted as well as she did. Not everyone would have the determination to go back to night school to get their high-school diploma. I think the boutique has been good for her, too."

Thomas closed his eyes briefly. The waiting silence inside of him suddenly fractured into hot, painful splinters of chaos. He realized how little he really knew Michelle. "Do you think so?" he asked, his voice sounding thick and strange.

Sam nodded, spooning creamer into his coffee. "It's the first thing she's ever had that's hers and hers alone. Oh, Patrick set her up in the beginning, but she paid him back. And Michelle has a unique style the tourists really seem to like, kind of a cross between Madonna and Alice in Wonderland. She tells me it's all luck, but she doesn't give herself credit. Adorn Me is a great little store. Michelle has even had offers to franchise, though she doesn't seem interested in expanding the business. Of course, I'm probably not telling you anything you don't know."

Thomas was silent for a moment, listening in a remote way to the sound of Sam's spoon clicking against his coffee cup. "What did you say the name of her store was?" he asked finally.

"Adorn Me. It's on Harrison, near the waterfront. You've never been down there?"

"No, not yet. But I intend to." Thomas didn't want the answer to his next question, but still he asked. "Michelle never told me when the big day was, Sam."

Sam found a nice banana in the fruit bowl. "What day? Oh, the wedding. That's still pretty much up in the air. You know Michelle—she likes to do things on impulse. It could be at noon today. It could be at noon two years from today. Whatever she decides."

What a patient fellow. "What about you? What do you want?"

Sam shrugged. "I want her to have what she wants," he said simply.

Thomas thought of the way Michelle had responded to his kisses, the hungry yearning in her dark eyes when he had pulled her robe aside and covered her tender flesh with his hands. Twenty minutes ago, Michelle had wanted Thomas Murphy.

"So do I," Thomas said. "So do I."

Ten minutes later, Michelle walked into a nightmare.

Thomas Murphy and Sam Hicks were sitting at the kitchen table sharing a cup of coffee. Thomas, the man who had very nearly ravished her on the kitchen floor that very morning, with her enthusiastic cooperation. And dear Sam, the man she had become engaged to just a week before. If there was any mercy in the situation at all, it was that Thomas had managed to find his shirt. He was also wearing a frilly apron.

"Omigosh," she said. The words were muttered, but both men heard her quite clearly. Heads turned; hazel eyes smiled cheerfully, blue eyes nailed her to the wall.

"Yes, Mick," Thomas said, settling back in his chair to enjoy the proceedings. "Omigosh Sam is here."

Sam rose, crossing the room to press a kiss on Michelle's cold cheek. "Good morning, sunshine. You look absolutely beautiful today."

Michelle looked like death warmed over, and she knew it. Her hair hung in an untidy braid over one shoulder, her jeans were a size too small, her sweatshirt three sizes too large and her blusher stood out on her waxen cheeks like war paint. Usually his relentless optimism was one of the qualities she adored most about Sam. At the moment, however, she found optimism as irritating to her raw nerves as sunlight and songbirds. "You're very kind," she said. "Have you and Thomas . . . have the two of you introduced yourselves?"

Sam nodded. "We have. Thomas was just telling me about his experiences in the boxing ring. It's fascinating."

Michelle looked at Thomas. "You were a fighter?" she asked faintly. "I didn't realize."

"Life is full of surprises," he replied in a creamy voice. "Especially around you, Mick. I hope Sam likes surprises. I have a feeling he's in for—"

She interrupted desperately. "Sam, I'm so sorry. We had a date to go house hunting this morning, didn't we? I'm afraid with all the excitement we've had around her lately—" her eyes touched on Thomas for a stinging second "—it completely slipped my mind. It won't take me a minute to get ready."

"We're in no rush," Sam offered kindly, apparently oblivious to the sexual and emotional tension shivering through the room. "We have all day. You know, Thomas mentioned how beautiful the wedding was. I can't tell you how badly I felt about missing it. I imagine it was an unforgettable night, knowing your father."

"Oh, it was . . . something," she said faintly.

"Wasn't it, though?" Thomas murmured, rearranging the fruit basket on the table with meticulous attention.

Sam nodded. "Thomas said the party went on until the wee hours of the morning. I wish I'd known. I got off work at midnight."

Thomas smiled at Michelle then, delivering a private little message with his heavy-lidded eyes. "Oh, the party really didn't get hopping until after midnight, did it, Mick?"

Michelle felt the heat building beneath her skin. Steaming. She tried to stare Thomas down, but her watering eyes were still painfully light sensitive. "Actually, things started to drag a little by then."

Thomas noted the ragged edge to her voice with vague satisfaction. He was in no mood to be chivalrous, not while he was sitting next to the lady's fiancé. "Anyway, what with one thing and another, I'm afraid a bit too much champagne was consumed. Poor Michelle found herself—"

"Trying to convince Thomas not to drive home in his bright-eyed condition," Michelle put in quickly. Her chin lifted fractionally, her red-rimmed eyes daring Thomas to contradict her. "Thomas does enjoy a good party, but he never knows when he's had enough. Anyway, he finally agreed to sleep it off here."

Thomas raked back his hair with his fingers and said nothing.

"Better safe than sorry," Sam replied. "You have no idea how many accident victims I see that are—" He was interrupted by a high-pitched signal from the pager on his belt. "Excuse me a moment. I need to call my service."

He used the kitchen phone, talking in quiet tones with his back to Michelle and Thomas. Michelle made the mistake of catching Thomas's eye. He gave her a sugary smile, patting the empty chair beside him. "Come sit down, sunshine."

Michelle did as she was told. In the circumstances, she thought it was prudent.

"Aren't you just a bundle of surprises," he said conversationally.

"Look, I would have told you last night, but I was too—"

"Drunk?" he supplied in a strange whisper, glancing furtively at Dr. Sam. "What a coincidence. So was I. At least, that's the story going around."

"I'm sorry. I don't know why I said that."

"Guilt? Panic? Embarrassment?" He tipped her chin up with his fingers. "Am I getting close? Why don't you wear a ring?"

"Sam gave me one, but it was too large. It's being sized."

"Mick Hicks. Catchy name."

"*He* calls me Michelle." He was so close, she could feel the heat of his body across the space between them. Her lips were dry. She wet them with the tip of her tongue, then her gaze drifted slowly, helplessly, to his mouth. "You and my father are the only ones who call me Mick."

He looked at her for a long moment. His eyes, bright in the soft light from the nearby window, were unexpectedly gentle. "That's something, at least."

Sam hung up the phone, sending Michelle an apologetic smile. "Here we go again. I'm afraid we'll have to postpone our house hunting, Michelle."

"The hospital?" she guessed, trying to sound disappointed. Well, of course she was disappointed. What was she thinking of? "Oh, Sam, I was really looking forward to going today."

"I thought you'd forgotten you were going today," Thomas murmured innocently.

She ignored Thomas, standing up and giving dear Sam a tight hug. Dear, reliable Sam. "Will you be long? We could go later."

"We could." Sam looked at his watch. "I'll try. I'll give you a call this afternoon."

"Only if you have time."

"I'll find the time. You don't mind waiting till later?"

"Not at all. Unless you'll be too tired?"

"I'll be fine. What about you?"

"Oh, I'm not tired at all."

Thomas slipped several inches lower in his chair, covering his eyes with his hand. Michelle and Sam reminded him of those two excruciatingly polite chipmunks from the cartoons . . . *After you. Oh, no, after you. Oh, I couldn't possibly. Please, I insist . . .*

It was almost too much to take on an empty stomach.

In the end, the good doctor and his hung-over fiancée compromised: they would have an early dinner at a restaurant they both enjoyed, and devote the following weekend to house hunting. Sam kissed Michelle goodbye—Thomas watched through his fingers, completely unimpressed by the man's technique—and departed with a cheerful wave. If it bothered him to leave Michelle alone with Thomas, he hid it very well.

The kitchen was filled with a dead silence after Sam left . . . but only for a moment.

"Hell of a nice guy," Thomas said. "He makes Mr. Rogers look like Attila the Hun."

Michelle gave the kitchen table a wide berth as she walked briskly to the refrigerator. "He's a wonderful man. Completely selfless. He would give you the shirt off his back if you asked."

"What about you?"

She ducked her head into the refrigerator, giving Thomas a wonderful view of soft denim stretched over round buttocks. "What about me?" she asked.

"Has he given you the shirt off his back? Or anything else off his person?"

Michelle rose too quickly, hitting her head on one of the shelves. "It's none of your business," she snapped. "Where's the orange juice?"

"I left it on the counter. You're awfully touchy about your love life, Mick."

She poured a glass of juice and took a healthy swallow before she answered. "My private life is just that—private."

"You're very different, you know—you and Dr. Kildare. He seems conservative. Mild-mannered. He probably wants a two-story colonial with a white picket fence and a twenty-year mortgage."

"As a matter of fact, he does." She put bread in the toaster, not because she wanted toast, but because it gave her something to do. "What's wrong with that? I've dreamed of a two-story colonial with a white picket fence and a twenty-year mortgage all my life, and everything else that comes along with it. Plastic lawn furniture. Tulips in the spring. A charcoal grill in the backyard."

How sad. Not once had she mentioned fig leaves or harmonicas or palm trees. "That sounds . . . nice." Nice . . . but completely lacking in island spice. He gave Michelle's fantasy a *C* minus.

"Oh, it will be better than nice," Michelle said. "It will be perfect."

"Does he play pool?"

Michelle began buttering the toast she didn't want. "Sam? No, he doesn't play pool."

"Oh, well . . . you should find a new hobby, anyway. Hustling pool games is a big no-no for doctors' wives." Then, when he could see the indignation flare in her eyes, he added quickly, "Golf! That's the ticket. Do you enjoy golfing?"

She despised golfing. She couldn't see the point in walking all over the golf course chasing after a ball that you had in your hands in the first place. "Just because I marry a doctor doesn't mean I have to play golf."

"Not too keen on golfing, are we? Too bad. Oh, well, you can always join a bridge club. How are you at bridge?"

She preferred five-card stud. "Oh, I'm *mad* about bridge," she replied brightly. "Aren't you sweet to be so concerned?"

"I'm a sweet guy. So how did you meet good old Sam?"

Michelle's headache was making a nasty comeback. She wondered what Thomas's record was for consecutive questions. "My hair caught in his zipper."

His eyes grew a little wider and, if possible, a little brighter. He sat up quite straight. "You aren't going to stop there, are you?"

"We were in an elevator in the hospital. I was visiting a friend; Sam was just coming to work. He was standing behind me, and when he unzipped his jacket, my hair got caught."

"And the rest is history. I do love a love story." He smiled then, and his voice became suddenly low, velvet soft. "So have you ever heard the one about the blonde in the pink leather skirt who walked into a bar and challenged the owner to a five-million-dollar pool game?"

Michelle bit her lip to control a tremor that seemed to begin deep in her soul. Why, oh, why couldn't she close the door he had opened for her? Every time he looked at her that way, her body felt a chill of desire and panic. Her first instinct was to fight, but how did she fight herself?

Deliberately she turned back on that seductive smile, peering inside the stainless-steel bowl on the counter. There was nothing like a dozen raw eggs to turn one's thoughts from temptation. "Are you going to do something with all these eggs you cracked?"

Thomas stood with easy, loose-limbed grace, dropping his frilly apron on the floor. Quietly he came up behind Michelle's stiff little figure, lifting a finger to tickle the flyaway hair at her nape. "Sweet Mick, prepare yourself. Before I go home today, I'm going to give you the most delectable experience of your young lifetime." Then, hearing her sudden intake of breath, he added sardonically, "Murphy's famous cheese omelet, baby. Just an omelet."

Five

—

"So, anyway, this strange guy calls me on the phone, and says that John gave him my number. Well, you know my brother John—he's always trying to set me up with these respectable types he thinks will calm me down. He thinks I'm frivolous. I think since John's a mortician, he's used to working with very quiet people, so I seem a little high-spirited in comparison. Well, anyway, I tell this guy— Leadbetter, he said his name was, Tim Leadbetter—sure, I'll go out to dinner with him, because I was broke and sick of macaroni and cheese and really wanted some red meat. I didn't tell him the part about being broke."

Bitsy McFairlane was steaming the wrinkles out of a new shipment of clothes while she filled Michelle in on her weekend. Bitsy was Michelle's part-time assistant at Adorn Me, a talkative Gypsy with a contagious Goldie Hawn giggle. She was twenty years old, with butchered auburn hair that she never allowed to grow more than an inch long, and enormous hazel eyes. She was a trial and a delight to all those who knew her.

"You actually told him you'd go out with him?" Michelle hit the wrong key on the calculator, wiping out thirty minutes of painstaking accounting. She hated Monday mornings, which was when she balanced Friday night's receipts. Math had never been one of her strong points, which was why she suffered through a night class in business accounting once a week. "Bitsy, I can't believe you'd agree to go out with some weird guy who just happened to call you on the phone one night!"

"I was hungry. Anyway, he wasn't some weird guy, he was a friend of John's." She reflected on this for a moment, frowning. "Come to think of it, all John's friends *are* pretty weird. Morticians really don't know how to mingle, you know what I mean?"

"Occupational hazard," Michelle murmured, her voice quavering slightly.

"Anyway, this Leadbetter says he'll pick me up about seven. So I get all dolled up, thinking John might surprise me this time, fix me up with somebody really hot. So, anyway, the doorbell rings at two minutes to seven. Now get this—when I open the door, there's this *old person* standing there. I swear, Michelle, the guy was at least forty-five years old."

Michelle was momentarily distracted, wondering how old Thomas Murphy might be. Younger than forty? Definitely. Older than thirty? Probably. Until he uncoiled the teasing smile that danced in his blue eyes and made him look all of seventeen. And why was she sitting here wondering how old Thomas Murphy was? Why did her mind keep jumping back to him like a magnet? Why had she subtracted seven percent from forty-two dollars and come up with sixteen hundred?

Michelle turned off her calculator and tossed it in her desk drawer. Obviously she was incapable of calculating anything this morning. "Forty-five isn't exactly ancient, Bitsy. Still, I can't believe John would fix you up with somebody twenty-five years older than you."

"He didn't," Bitsy replied, giggling. "Leadbetter and I got to talking, and he said how I didn't look a thing like John had described to him. Anyway, we finally figured out that *his* John and *my* John were two different people. Leadbetter had an attorney friend named John who had given him a phone number of some divorcée. The poor guy dialed the number wrong and got me instead!"

Michelle stared at her, wavering between astonishment and laughter. "What on earth did you do?"

"We went out to dinner," Bitsy said matter-of-factly. "I had veal oscar." She held up a finger, listening as door chimes sounded in the front of the store. "Hark, there's our first customer of the day."

"I'll go," Michelle said, pushing her chair back from her desk. "Meanwhile, do me a favor and burn all the ledger books, will you?" Then, as a precaution, she added with a bright smile, "Just kidding, Bitsy. Just kidding."

Adorn Me was a very small store, and extremely crowded with a startling selection of merchandise. There were antique clothes and designer clothes, handmade quilts, original watercolors and a fascinating collection of cuckoo clocks. There were hanging things and feathery things and skimpy, glittery things—everything and anything that had ever caught Michelle's whimsical eye. She loved the barely organized chaos of her store, especially when four dozen cuckoo clocks came alive every hour on the hour. It kept the customers on their toes.

Michelle glanced at her watch as she ducked around the Japanese screen that divided her "office" from the rest of the store. It was only ten o'clock in the morning, but it seemed as if she'd been at the books for hours and hours, and accomplished nothing. The muscles that Thomas had tied into knots forty-eight hours earlier still thrummed with tension. She couldn't rid herself of the stubborn, strange anticipation that constantly distracted her.

Damn, he made her mad.

A teenage boy was standing at the front counter, wrestling with a feather boa that had dropped from an overhead shelf. He wore a drab brown uniform and carried a long white florist's box beneath his arm.

"Can I help you?" Michelle asked, relieving him of his boa.

"Yeah...thanks. For a minute there, I thought it was alive. Uh, I'm looking for—" he consulted his clipboard "—DeMara. Mick DeMara. Is he here?"

"*She's* here," Michelle said, trying and failing to keep her voice steady. Flowers. Flowers were romantic, impractical, extravagant...not at all her style. Why were her hands shaking as she signed for them? And why on earth couldn't she remember how to spell her own name?

Bitsy brought an armful of hand-painted smocks from the back room just as the delivery boy left. "Heigh-ho, who was that? Never mind, he was too young for me. I only go for men with receding hairlines these days. Michelle, m'dear, what have you there? Ooooh, flowers? Dr. Sammy sent you flowers?"

Michelle swallowed hard and lifted the lid off the box. To her amazement, she found a rainbow-colored flower lei inside. A gorgeous necklace of lush orchids and mysterious tropical flowers, the kind that made you think of grass skirts and swaying palms and warm trade winds. The enclosed card wasn't signed, but then it didn't need to be: *Life is full of surprises.*

"What on earth...?" Bitsy was confused, but impressed. "I've never seen orchids that big."

"It's a lei," Michelle said blankly, lifting the heavy garland out of the box.

"Well, I know it's a lei. I've been to Hawaii before. The tour guide threw one of those things around my neck at the airport. But it was plastic." Bitsy whistled through her front teeth. "I tell you, that really takes imagination. Who would have thought Dr. Sammy would do something like this? I would have pegged him as a red rose kind of guy. You know, more traditional."

Michelle buried her nose in the flowers and inhaled an exotic, sweet-scented rain forest. For me, she thought, with shock waves of emotion running through her nervous system. What a strange, whimsical, funny thing to do.

"I wonder how you would water it?" Bitsy mused thoughtfully, looking at the lei like it was a pet that needed to be cared for. "Maybe we should float it in the bathroom sink or something."

Michelle looked at her earnest little assistant and came back down to earth with a jarring thud. This was crazy. She was acting as if a man had never sent her flowers before.

Which was true, if truth be told. But beside the point. Thomas Murphy had no business making her feel special.

She placed the lei over Bitsy's shorn head. "There. It looks nice on you. Wear it with my blessings and get back to work."

"But won't Sam expect you to—"

"Sam has nothing to do with this," Michelle said.

Mischief gleamed in Bitsy's eyes. "Oh, my. Oh, *my*. There's another rooster in the henhouse, is there? Look, I know it's probably none of my business, but—"

"If I were you," Michelle said sweetly, "I'd go with that instinct."

Thomas gave a great deal of thought to what he was going to wear that day. Actually, he was surprised at himself. In the past, his attire had never been a big point with him. His clothes were always comfortable, always casual and occasionally ironed. He'd never worried whether his shirt brought out the color of his eyes or if his jeans were fraying at the seams. He had an athlete's body, broad shoulders sloping into narrow hips, and he knew most things looked fairly decent on him.

But fairly decent wasn't good enough. Not today. He'd sent flowers to Michelle at her boutique that morning, not boring red roses like everybody sent everybody, but an exotic lei. The florist had thought his request was a little crazy, and it had ended up costing him more than five dozen roses would have, but it was worth it. He'd ordered masses of perfumed pink, yellow and white frangipani, hibiscus, orchids and gardenias. Thomas loved the mystical, intoxicating scents of tropical flowers. They opened up a fresh universe of sensual pleasures. In his opinion, French perfumers could learn a great deal from the natural fragrances of the "primitive world."

Yes, a stroke of creative genius, those flowers. Sam Hicks would never have thought of it. And Thomas intended to follow them up with a friendly visit to the store, just to remind sweet Mick he was alive and breathing heavily. He knew she'd been thrown off balance by the powerful chemistry between them, and her defenses would be stronger than ever. He knew she had a fiancé, and fully intended on marrying him. He knew she was going to fight Thomas Alexander Murphy every inch of the way.

He could hardly wait.

In the end he decided on khaki pleated slacks and a colorful Hawaiian-print shirt that fit his tropical mood very nicely. He thought about getting a much-needed haircut, but decided against it. He didn't want to look as if he was trying too hard. He *was* trying too hard for that. Besides, his barber was frightening. The fellow couldn't seem to grasp the concept of "a little off the sides." There would be no barbers allowed on Thomas's someday island.

He walked into Adorn Me at 6:00 p.m. that evening. His arrival seemed to set off some sort of musical catastrophe. The entire store suddenly erupted in a startling, jangling explosion of sound and movement. Birds came in and out of little houses on the walls, peeping and chirping. Gongs and chimes sounded, again and again and again. Thomas covered his ears and leaned his hip on the front counter and thought, Only you, Mick.

Michelle came bounding to the front, a pencil stuck behind her ear and a huge black scarf tied in her hair. She was wearing a most interesting outfit—black tights, red ballet shoes and a scarlet T-shirt that reached to her knees, studded here, there and everywhere with sparkly things. A very "Mick" sort of look. He drank her in until the cuckoo commotion died down.

"Why, oh, why can't I visualize you as a doctor's wife?" Thomas asked cheerfully, his eyes running the length of her with thoroughly masculine appreciation.

"Thomas," she said faintly, staring into the periwinkle-blue eyes that were as thickly lashed as her own. How could a man look so...manly...wearing hot-pink gardenias all over his shirt? It probably had something to do with the square shoulders and the triceps and the pectorals and all other beautifully shaped things beneath those hot-pink gardenias.

"You remember," Thomas said with a sunny smile. "I'm flattered. You're looking very fetching today, lamb chop. What are those things in your ears?"

Automatically Michelle's hand went to her earrings. "Oh. Seashells. What are you doing here?"

His wry look told her what a ridiculous question she'd just asked. They both knew exactly why he was here. Still, if she was more comfortable playing innocent, he was willing. Anything for the lady with the seashells in her ears. "Good old Sam told me about your store. I wanted to see it for myself." His lively gaze wandered reluctantly away from Michelle, taking in the wild variety of clothing and merchandise. An irresistible combination of sophistication and simplicity, whimsy and flash. "He really didn't do it justice. I've never seen anything quite like this."

"Well...*aloha*!" This from Bitsy, who had just appeared behind the cash register. She'd been on her knees behind the counter rearranging boxes when Thomas had come in. "A festive shirt you have on there, sir. Are you taken? I mean—" she cleared her throat "—have you been helped?"

Nothing about this store could surprise him, Thomas thought with a wave of amusement. Not even this redheaded, new-wave Gidget...who just happened to be wearing his lei. "I'm helping myself," he said. "And may I say that's a unique and incredibly tasteful floral arrangement you're wearing."

Bitsy made a soft "ahem," coloring beneath her tan. "Yeah, well...thank you. It's borrowed, I'm afraid. Why do I get the feeling you already know that?" Then, in a stage whisper to Michelle, "This is the rooster, right?"

Michelle closed her eyes tightly for a moment and then opened them again. "Bitsy, why don't you go home now? I'll close the store tonight."

Bitsy grinned and took off the lei, dropping it neatly over Michelle's head. "It looks better on you, anyway. Goes with your earrings."

"Good night, Bitsy."

Bitsy pouted good-naturedly, picking up her purse from behind the counter. "First Leadbetter, then this. I swear, fate has it in for me. I'm just not meant to have any fun. Can you at least tell me your name?" This last question was addressed to Thomas.

"My name is Thomas Alexander Murphy," he said amiably, still holding Michelle's eyes. "And guess what? I'm going to make your boss an extremely satisfied woman."

Bitsy whimpered a little and walked out the door, taking down the Open sign as she went.

"That wasn't funny," Michelle said. "Bitsy and Sam are friends. What do you think she's going to tell him?"

Thomas frowned and ran his hand through his thick hair. "I don't know her too well, but she really doesn't seem like the type we can trust to keep our tempestuous love affair a secret."

Michelle's smile said he wasn't going to fluster her. "We're not having a tempestuous love affair," she said. "You must have me confused with someone else."

"It would be impossible to confuse you with anyone else," Thomas replied, flicking her seashell earrings with his index finger. They clinked and jingled together like a row of miniature wind chimes. "You're one of a kind, kid. It's good to see you again, by the way."

It's good to see you, too, Michelle thought, but she wasn't about to say it. One way or another, she had to get a handle on this situation. She was very good at saving herself, she always had been. And now she was determined to save herself from Thomas Murphy. She knew his type—the funloving answer to a maiden's prayers, as long as the maiden prayed for nothing more serious than a whale of a good time. She wasn't prepared emotionally for a "close your eyes and jump" love affair. At heart she was a weary romantic, guarding secret, wistful dreams of how life should be...but seldom was. She wanted to fill the future with things that belonged to her and her alone, things she could cherish and depend on. Dear, sweet Sam. Children, at least five or six. And, yes, the two-story colonial.

Substance. And there was no substance in the eye of Thomas Murphy's sensual hurricane. She wasn't going to set aside everything she needed and wanted to chase after rainbows in his honor.

"I'm not going to play your game, Thomas," she said, trying to keep her voice neutral. "We don't have any secrets together. You're not helping yourself to anything. And you're not going to make me a satisfied woman." There, she'd made everything perfectly clear to him. And to herself, she thought, fighting an inexplicable wave of sadness. "So... I guess that's that."

Thomas pulled a face. "I should have sent you a cactus."

"You're impossible!" Then, belatedly, "The lei is beautiful. Thank you."

"You're welcome. If it was so beautiful, why did you give it away?"

She buried her chin in the fragrant blooms. Silence fell between them like a brick.

"Did you know the most primitive, basic sense we have is the sense of smell?" Thomas asked softly. His eyes had become brighter, coaxing. "It's true. Experts say the sense of smell is the last to leave us when we die, and the one most strongly related to emotion."

Michelle closed her eyes, inhaling the fragrance of gentle winds blowing through lush island gardens. Irresistibly caught in a web of seductive, exotic smells, she let her imagination wander through a languorous and sensual paradise. A warm, white-sand beach. Heavy, sweet-scented air. Hothouse lushness crowding tin-roofed cottages. And a man, brown as a berry, with long, sun-streaked hair and a dazzling pirate's smile. Yes. She could picture Thomas there, giving himself completely to the unhurried days and sultry tropical nights.

As he watched her, he could see the slight furrowing of her brow, as if she were concentrating. Her face tilted slightly, her chin rubbing against a waxy white gardenia, her silky lashes soft shadows against her skin. He felt an intense, dreamy pleasure in her, in everything about her. "What do you see?" he asked, moving closer. "Tell me."

She opened her eyes, wide and bright. "Trouble," she said flatly, deliberately forestalling his attempt to take her into his arms. She took off the lei and placed it around the neck of a smiling mannequin wearing a genuine fish-scale bikini. "With a capital *T*."

Thomas's lower lip jutted out and his eyes reproached. "Why do women always confuse enjoyment with trouble?"

She sniffed skeptically. "You mean there's a difference?"

"Maybe not." He grinned. "Come to dinner with me tonight and we'll find out."

"You didn't listen to a word I said!"

"Not true, my troublesome friend with a capital *T*. I heard every single syllable." He stepped forward, and she stepped backward, into a circular rack of jackets.

Her hands went behind her to steady herself, her palms closing in tight fists over soft leather. And she held on to that leather for dear life as Thomas bent his head, his lips brushing a smile on the side of her neck through a silky net of pale hair.

"We don't have any secrets," he whispered, his breath tickling the sensitive folds of her ear. His hands closed over her slight waist, then moved slowly down the sides of her hips, pulling her tightly into the warm cradle of his thighs. "I'm not helping myself to anything."

Now his eyes were softer, warmer, more intense, focused on her mouth. Again he bent his head, catching her lower lip softly between his teeth, sucking gently. Tasting her. Tormenting her with the light, knowing motions of his tongue and mouth before possessing her completely with a kiss that was hard and possessive and demanding. A kiss he broke from wide-eyed and trembling, just as she did.

"And I'm not going to make you a satisfied woman." He gasped, resting his forehead against hers and closing his eyes until his heart found a steady rhythm once again. "See? I've been very attentive."

It was a tribute to her willpower that her white-knuckled fingers still clutched at the leather jacket behind her. She wanted desperately to touch him. She wanted to discover the texture of his flesh, the beautiful play of his muscles over bone and sinew. His energy, his humor, his breezy sensuality, teased her imagination. And his experience. He was so vital, vibrating with electricity...but still. So still, just...waiting. She was acutely aware of his mouth so close to hers, his breath whispering over her lips.

"That wasn't fair," she whispered hoarsely.

"I know," he said, lifting his head to smile down into her eyes. "But it sure felt good."

"And that's all that matters?"

"Oh, Mick...you think too much, do you know that? It's not good for you." And then he surprised her, backing away, turning his attention to the leather coats like any other interested shopper. He circled the rack slowly, pushing hangers this way and that, touching the soft leather. "I used to have a coat like this one," he said suddenly, pulling a black leather bomber jacket off the hanger. "When I was...I don't know, sixteen or seventeen. I wore it all the time, summer and winter. I thought it made me look tough."

Michelle followed him with her eyes, still wary. "Were you?"

"Tough?" He shrugged into the jacket, his smile stretching to a wicked grin. "Hell, yes—how could you even ask?"

She could see it in him, Michelle thought, the boy he once was. His honey-colored hair was tangled across his forehead, defining the wild blue of his eyes. His hips moved with a lazy masculine rhythm as he walked to the full-length mirror to look at the jacket. Her mouth went dry. For a moment she was caught between what he once was and what he had become, and there was a very fine line between the two.

"Where did you grow up?" she asked softly, watching his face in the mirror. Knowing it was dangerous to learn any more about him.

He laughed and pushed his hands in the pockets of the jacket, looking impossibly young and appealing. "I'd love to be able to wring your heart with an address like Hell's Kitchen, but I spent the first fifteen years of my life in Chickasha, Oklahoma. Lots of fresh air, sunshine, nifty stuff like that.''

Chickasha. It didn't sound like a breeding ground for rebels in black leather jackets. ''What happened when you were fifteen?''

''I left,'' he said, meeting her eyes through the chill medium of the mirror. ''My mother died. She had a bad heart, so it wasn't unexpected. My dad and I had never gotten along, so there was no reason to stick around. It was a mutual agreement.''

A moment of quiet passed before she spoke. She was careful to keep the pity out of her voice. She could only go by her own instincts, but pity was frightening to her, abhorrent. Something told her it was the same with him. ''Where did you go?''

''New York. I'd always been pretty good in a boxing ring, so I figured I was destined for fame and fortune. If I wasn't looking for a fight on the street, I was in the gym looking for one. After a while I got tired of getting my nose broken, so I decided there might be a few things I still had to learn about fighting. A friend of mine had an uncle who was a trainer, and he took me in hand. Once I started training seriously for the amateur circuit, I was too tired to raise much hell.'' He turned, taking in her carefully arranged expression with a gentle smile. The air was warm and heavy with emotions, but different ones now, gentler. ''There's a reason I told you all this, by the way. Neither of us have lived a traditional life. I thought it might make you feel better if you realized we had a few things in common.''

His smile gave her absolutely no reassurance. ''Better about what?''

''Us,'' he said.

Michelle closed her eyes briefly, trying to find something familiar and stable inside. There was nothing. ''I don't know how I can make you understand," she said finally. "There is no us. There never will be."

"My adorable coward, there has been an 'us' since the first time I saw you toss a peanut in your mouth." He took off the jacket, replacing it on the hanger. "I've outgrown black leather, thank God," he said, putting the coat back on the rack. "Fighting for fun and profit isn't everything it's cracked up to be. I'm into fig leaves and harmonica music these days."

"Fig leaves." Her tone indicated she thought he might have taken one too many blows to the head.

Smiling, he wandered over to the bikini-clad mannequin wreathed in tropical flowers. He couldn't help but wonder what his curvaceous pool shark would look like in fish scales. "I'll tell you a secret, Mick," he said. "One day, in the not-so-distant future, I'm going to sell Shenanigans and clean out my savings account and buy a stretch of beach on a sun-drenched tropical island. There I will go barefoot every day and practise my harmonica and collect conch shells. You're welcome to join me."

She stared at him for what seemed to be a long, long time. She could have sworn he was perfectly serious, both about the purchase of his island hideaway and the invitation to join him there. "You're an exhausting man," she said finally.

"Exhaustion can be fun. Give it a chance."

"There's more to life than having fun."

"Not if you're lucky. Will you come to dinner with me tonight?"

"I have plans tonight."

"How about the El Bambi café? It's a dive, but they make unbelievable crab nachos."

"I'm *engaged*, Thomas."

"I just asked to feed you," he said, "not marry you. Engaged people eat, I know they do. We can have a friendly dinner together with no harm done. I would be a very good boy, I promise.''

Michelle looked into his eyes and he looked into hers. She was acutely conscious of the yearning in his gaze, of the quiet tension in his muscles, the slightly arrhythmic sound of his breathing. The desire was there between them, and there was no getting away from it. "No, you wouldn't," she said softly.

His smile was faint. "No, maybe I wouldn't." Something he saw in her face made his eyes grow darker as he took a step toward her. "But good intentions ought to count for something..."

Before Michelle knew what was happening, she was in his arms, and his lips were sweet and warm on hers. At first the kiss was gentle and undemanding, but within seconds they were both wild with need, completely out of control. She wrapped her arms around his neck and he cupped his hands over her buttocks, lifting her off the ground. The spiraling hunger they experienced shattered all their differences. Michelle was breathless, digging her hands into his hair and drinking in his kisses. She arched her back, pressing into him, trying to absorb as much of him as she could. But with every kiss, the hollow aching inside grew worse, emptier, more painful, and soon she couldn't bear it any longer. She released her grasp around his neck with a muttered protest, and slowly he lowered her to her feet.

"I can't," she moaned distractedly. "Thomas...we have to stop this..."

"We might have a problem there," he said huskily. "When this kind of thing happens between two people, it generally gets harder and harder to stop."

She pushed away from him, feeling lonely, fragile, needy...dangerously incapable of saving herself. "I suppose you're speaking from experience," she said in a small, tight voice, touching her palms to her cheeks. Her skin was hot.

There was panic and resentment, as well as desire, in her eyes. His heart, usually so hale and hearty, suddenly felt constricted. He'd never meant to overwhelm her, or push her into a relationship she wasn't prepared for. He needed more from her than a reluctant surrender. He realized she needed more time to understand and accept what was happening between them, and some of the tenderness he felt went into his soft smile. "Lady," he said quietly, "I've never experienced anything like you in my life. And sooner or later we're going to have to do something about this. You know that, don't you?"

She didn't have the energy to pretend to misunderstand him. She stuffed her hands in the deep pockets of her shirt, saying nothing. She stared at him, completely at a loss for words. Her pulse seemed permanently lodged in her throat.

Presently Thomas murmured, "You've no idea how humbling it is to see that petrified look on your face. And now that I've swept you off your feet with my irresistible charm, I think I'll be on my way." And then he grinned, shaking his head. "Damn but you're beautiful."

She watched him walk away, her eyes dark and helpless. He paused in the doorway, looking back at her, then smiled and shook his head once again before closing the door softly behind him.

Michelle listened to the door chimes fade into silence. She touched her fingers to her lips and felt tiny chills shiver down her spine. Her hand moved to her breast, absorbing the frantic dance of her heart.

"Oh, dear," she whispered.

Michelle had a late dinner date with Sam that same evening. The timing was unfortunate. Michelle was running scared, and she desperately wanted reassurance that her physical response to Thomas was largely Mother Nature's handiwork. Not only was the man impossibly good-looking, but he knew all the right buttons to push. Given the time, he could probably wring tears of pleasure from a granite stone. Michelle was young and healthy and just as susceptible to basic urges as the next person. No doubt Sam—a man she truly cared for—could inspire those same passionate feelings. No doubt at all. Up until this point their relationship had been lighthearted and undemanding—two devoted friends who had all the time in the world to become lovers. Pleasant, uncomplicated and very comfortable.

Suddenly Michelle had a good idea of what she might have been missing.

Without consciously examining her motives, she found herself taking extraordinary care with her appearance that night. She unearthed a strapless red silk dress in the back of her closet that clung in all the right places, and a few of the wrong places, as well. She toned down her earrings to three simple pearl studs, knowing that Sam found her more extravagant jewelry a little distracting. She doused herself liberally in his favorite perfume, blushing rosy red when she anointed the shadowed cleft between her breasts. Had she thought about it, she would have likened her ritual to that of a sacrificial lamb being readied for the slaughter. But she was very careful not to think about it.

Sam came directly from the hospital to the house, and smelled rather strongly of antiseptic. He apologized and she forgave him, pressing a kiss directly on his lips and leaving a glossy scarlet stain there. She laughed uneasily and tried to wipe it off with her fingers. Perhaps she'd overdone the lipstick.

"I'll do it," Sam said, taking a handkerchief from his jacket pocket. While he rubbed at his mouth, he took in the red silk dress. His eyes stretched above the handkerchief and a flush jumped out like slap marks on his high cheekbones.

"I think I need to sit down," he said when he was free of lipstick. "That dress of yours takes my breath away."

"I haven't worn it for ages," Michelle said, wondering if she ought to mention the smear of lipstick on his front tooth. "It seemed perfect for tonight, though. I wanted to look extra-special for you."

Sam looked confused, then glanced at his watch for the date. "What have I forgotten? It's not your birth—no, that's in December. I can't have missed an anniversary, we're not married yet." He frowned suddenly. "Unless you're the type who celebrates the six-month anniversary of the first day we held hands, that sort of thing? Did I forget something terribly romantic?"

"Don't be stupid. You know me better than that." Then she flushed, uncomfortably aware that not only had she snapped at him, but she had just called him stupid. She didn't want to snap at Sam tonight. She wanted everything to be absolutely perfect. It was terribly important. "I just wanted to look nice for you, that's all. I want you to know that I would never take you for granted, Sam. You're a wonderful person, the most thoughtful and considerate man I've ever met in my life." She tried on a flirtatious smile. "Not to mention incredibly good-looking."

Sam looked at her blankly. "Is it *my* birthday?"

She shrugged, nearly losing the top of the red silk dress. She would have to be very careful not to take any deep breaths tonight. "That all depends. There are birthdays, and there are birthdays."

He loosened his tie and said they had dinner reservations for nine.

Michelle ate very little that night. She thoughtfully questioned Sam about the operation he had observed that afternoon and was rewarded with an enthusiastic snip-by-snip account. Sam truly loved his chosen profession, and it didn't bother him at all to fondly reminisce while digging into clam linguini. Michelle sipped at her water and nodded in all the right places, trying to look—and feel—utterly fascinated. She told herself she would get used to this, that the day would come when she could cheerfully discuss a bowel resection while she enjoyed a nice plate of pasta right along with her husband.

By the time Sam pulled his Wagoneer into the huge circular driveway at Cliff Road, her stomach had settled. When he moved to open the car door, she stopped him with her hand on his arm. "Let's not go in yet," she said softly. "Let's talk for a few minutes."

He looked sideways at her, then shrugged and sat back in his seat. "All right. What would you like to talk about?"

"Well...actually, I wanted to ask you something." She smiled and shook back her hair. Trying to feel wild, abandoned. "I'd like you to kiss me, Sam."

He smiled in the darkness. "I was sort of saving it for later, but if you insist..." He leaned toward her, kissing her lightly, gently, on the lips. When he drew back, he was still smiling. "Happy to oblige, ma'am."

"Not like that," Michelle said, an edge of frustration to her voice. "Like *this*." She grabbed him by the shoulders, dragging his face down to hers. She kissed him with a desperation born of panic, trying to feel a hint, a shred, of the fiery magic she had felt with Thomas. She felt warm and cozy, but that she could achieve with thermal underwear. She wanted more. She wanted fireworks. She wanted skyrockets, catherine wheels, firecrackers...

She wanted Thomas.

When the kiss finally ended, Sam was staring at her with startled green eyes, and the silence in the car was deafening. "They taught us all about this in medical school," he said finally, tucking a strand of her hair clumsily behind her ear. "Hormones. Women have these hormones, and they become dangerous. You're one of the most dangerous women I've ever met in my life, Michelle DeMara."

She almost cried. Sam was thinking of her, as always, trying to make her feel more comfortable in an extremely awkward situation. She turned her head away from him, blinking away the sudden tears. What on earth had gotten into her? Thomas Murphy had shaken her self-confidence, shattered her defenses and aroused wild longings. And she, naive little dimwit she was, had tried to justify her enthusiastic cooperation by pinning it on Mother Nature.

When she could trust her voice, she said huskily, "I'm so sorry. That wasn't fair."

"We're going to be in a lot of trouble if you apologize every time you kiss me," Sam said teasingly. "Believe me, I can bear up under the strain. Feel free to give into these urges at any time."

She did kiss him then, a brief, sexless kiss on the cheek. "Thank you, Sam."

"For what?"

"Just being you. You're very special." It was enough, she told herself. It was more than enough.

Sam grinned. "It comes naturally."

He walked her to the front door in the hazy light of a full moon. Then he looked down into her eyes, and whatever he saw there made him pull her to him in a gentle, comforting hug. He didn't ask to come inside. Sam always seemed to know when she needed to be alone. "Sweet dreams," he whispered, touching his lips to her forehead.

Michelle remained on the marble steps, waiting until the sound of the Wagoneer's engine was lost in the murmur of the ocean. As always, she was reluctant to venture inside the house. She hated all that vast, empty space around her. She felt more welcome outside, blanketed with the stars and the moonlight and the soothing night wind. She sat down on the top step and lifted her face to the sky. Starlight drifted down on her, tangling in her hair and her eyes. Almost as bright and comforting as her night-light.

Everything was going to be all right, she told herself firmly. Thomas Murphy was no longer a stranger to her, never would be again, but he wasn't necessary to her happiness. Actually, she wasn't even sure she liked him very much. He was awfully full of himself, too self-confident for his own good—not to mention hers. He brought her new restlessness, which she didn't need. He promised her adventure, which she didn't want. And as for satisfaction...she knew herself well enough to realize that physical excitement could never fill the gnawing emptiness deep inside of her.

For the first time in her life, she had it all in sight—a home, a husband, a place in the world where she would truly belong. And more importantly, a man who would never hurt her. Patient, reliable Sam, who understood her so well, who would make all her happy-ever-after dreams come true. Finally.

Yes, everything was going to be all right...if she could only remember who she was and who Thomas was and why the twain should never, ever meet. If she could stop wondering all the time about the wild magic he had in his eyes and his hands and his smile. If she could shrug off the clumsy, virginal daydreams that made her feel so bewildered and anxious and full of nothing but him.

Virginal. She couldn't help wondering how many women could claim that dubious honor at the ripe old age of twenty-four. No wonder her hormones were turning on her. They were dying of curiosity.

She sighed, watching the moon turn over in its sleep behind a wispy cloud. Sometimes being a survivor was a lonely business.

Six

A restless woman with too much time on her hands was capable of almost anything.

Saturday morning found Michelle lying in the cramped space between the driveway and her Mazda, studying the belly of the car. It looked simple enough—she would drain the oil out of the car *there*—at least, she thought it was there—then pull out the old oil filter and pop in a new one. Then it was just a matter of going under the hood and finding the right place to pour the new oil in. Who needed a gas station when you were industrious and determined and bored out of your skull?

"Piece of cake," she said aloud, wiping her hands on her overalls in preparation.

"Famous last words," a familiar disembodied male voice replied.

Michelle turned her head slowly, wincing as she saw a pair of battered white tennis shoes twelve inches from her nose.

Life was so unfair. You'd think a woman would be safe underneath her very own car. "Thomas?"

"Yes, cupcake. And it looks like I got here in the nick of time. What do you think you're doing under there?"

It could have been such a nice day, Michelle thought despairingly. If Sam hadn't been called to do a double shift at the hospital, she would have been house hunting right now. Safely out of temptation's path and happily seeking the two-story colonial of her dreams. "I'm going to change the oil in my car."

A soft whistle. "Oh, boy. First time?"

"Yes," she told his shoes. "But there has to be a first time for everything."

He came down on his haunches, then leaned sideways to peer beneath the car. His face was nearly upside down, his hair falling away from his forehead in a silky tangle. He wore a white T-shirt that skimmed the muscles of his chest and shoulders, and held a bright yellow baseball cap in his hand. "That's the first encouragement you've given me, Mick."

"I was talking about the car."

"I wasn't." He grinned, a lazy light twinkling in his eyes. "Why don't I crawl under there and give you the benefit of my experience? I'm really good in tight places."

"I work alone," Michelle muttered, experiencing the same tightness in her chest that seemed to plague her whenever he was around. Her instinct was to remain right where she was, protected from charm and harm in her cramped little space. If she had had a paper bag, she would have pulled it over her head.

"That's your problem. You don't understand the principle of teamwork, cupcake. But you will." And then he was shimmying in beside her, thigh to thigh, shoulder to shoulder. "This is much better," he said, grinning at her startled expression. "Now I can talk you through the whole thing and you won't do anything silly like draining out the transmission fluid. Don't thank me. I love to feel needed."

It wasn't a romantic atmosphere. The dark shadows were thick with the odors of gasoline and oil. There was no room to move, sandwiched between the hard concrete and the grimy underside of the Mazda. Still, Michelle was intensely conscious of the erotic pressure of his hip against hers, of the not-so-subtle invitation in that crooked, trust-me smile that had haunted her waking and her sleeping. Her body began to react as if they were sharing a comfortable double bed.

"You're crowding me," she said, straight from the heart.

"Yeah." He looked dreamy-eyed and slightly reckless. "Like I said, I'm at my best in tight places." He kissed a smile against her shoulder, and his lips burned straight through the denim overalls she wore. "So tell me, my little grease monkey... have you missed me like crazy?"

Seduction under a Mazda. Michelle decided that Thomas Murphy was capable of anything. She turned her head away from him, staring at the mass of confusion that was an engine. "There are no words to describe the unutterable loneliness I have suffered," she said, putting a cloying overdose of emotion into her voice. "Look there—is that the bolt to the oil pan?"

He sighed. "You're a tough proposition, honey."

"A losing proposition, honey," she said. It was a good thing he couldn't see how her hands were shaking—he'd know just how "tough" she really was. She was no proof against that crestfallen little-boy huskiness in his voice. Oh, he was good in tight places, all right. Wouldn't it be wonderful if he took her at her word and finally accepted defeat?

Wouldn't it?

"It's a good thing I thrive on a challenge," Thomas said, looking at her with a critical eye.

She wriggled closer to the tire on her right. "If that's the case, I'll surrender on the spot."

"That's the spirit! I wish you had bought an American-made car, though. They're a little higher off the ground. Oh, well, I'm game. Cuddle up."

There would be no oil change for the little Mazda today, Michelle decided. She scrambled out from the cramped space, shielding her eyes from the late-summer sun as she got to her feet. He frustrated her to death, she told herself angrily, and made her want things she shouldn't want, she told herself sadly.

"I'll do it later," she said.

Thomas was right behind her, brushing the dust off blue jeans faded almost to white. "I can't stand the suspense. Do what, pray tell?"

Michelle raised her eyes to his, steeling herself as the familiar jolt of electricity sparked through her nerve endings. How unfair that one man should have such power over the opposite sex. His smile was a wicked invitation. His eyes were narrowed against the glare of the sun, hot blue and mischievous. The light breeze took his long hair in a hundred different directions at once, tumbling ivory over gold over brown. "Change the oil in the car," she said. "Has anyone ever told you your imagination runs on a very predictable—not to mention horizontal—track?"

He grinned, apparently taking her remarks as a compliment. "Has anyone ever told you how fetching you look in a pair of baggy overalls? Still, I'd love to see you in less. Let's go to the beach and frolic."

"What . . . now?"

He picked up his baseball cap from the driveway and fit it over his tangled hair. "No—on September sixteenth of next year. Idiot, of course *now*. Run in the house and take off all your many earrings and grab a suit."

Automatically Michelle's hand went to her earlobe. She was wearing colorful wooden parrots today, red enamel hoops and tiny silver lightning bolts. "I'm not taking off my earrings." She wasn't taking off anything around him. An ounce of prevention and three yards of heavy denim were worth a pound of cure. "And I'm not going to the beach today. I can't go anywhere. It's going to rain, and besides, Sam's going to call me when he gets off duty. We're going house hunting."

"And when does Dr. Sammy get off?"

Actually, he didn't get off until midnight. Fortunately Michelle knew how to bluff with the best of them. "I'm not sure. It's kind of up in the air."

"Aren't we all," Thomas murmured. He set a parrot to swinging with a flick of his index finger. "Don't be difficult, Mick. Pretty please."

Her lips compressed in a stubborn line. "I was born difficult."

"If you turn me down, I might find someone else to go play with."

The thought of Thomas Murphy frolicking on the beach with another woman was unpleasant. Repulsive, even. Michelle would have walked on hot coals before she admitted it, though. "Don't forget your sunscreen," she said sweetly, then turned and began walking across the lawn toward the house.

Behind her Thomas made clucking noises. *"Chicken"* noises. She stopped in her tracks, feeling his eyes burning into her back. "Stop that right now."

"If the shoe fits..."

She turned back to him defiantly. "Why aren't you married, Thomas?"

She'd taken him completely by surprise. "What?"

"I said, why aren't you married?"

She was waiting for an answer. This was truly dirty pool, Thomas thought, turning a full-of-possibilities summer's day into a sobering discussion of holy matrimony. His shiver was inappropriate for the comfortable August weather. "Should I be married?"

"Well, at your age, which is probably somewhere between thirty and forty, but I can't say for sure because you're too sensitive about it to tell me...at your age, most men have outgrown their lustful adolescence and are mature enough to handle a permanent relationship."

"Lustful adolescence?" Thomas began to walk toward her with lazy intent. "Why, Mick, I didn't realize you were such an authority on men. I'm impressed."

Michelle swallowed hard, immediately regretting her bold move. If the discussion was going to take a nasty turn toward her experience with men, she had best retreat with all possible speed. "Never mind. It's really none of my business."

He came closer, pushing up the brim of his cap with his thumb. "I have a great idea, cupcake. Let's not have any secrets from each other. I'll tell you why I've never married, and you tell me where you got all your vast experience with the opposite sex. You first."

Her eyes were level with his crooked grin. Somehow in the past five seconds, she'd completely lost her advantage. "You're being ridiculous."

"I'm sorry." He brought his body inch by inch against hers. Slowly...slowly. "I guess I'm still in my lustful adolescent stage."

Michelle closed her eyes, struggling to enforce the crumbling hold on her willpower. "Thomas..."

"Mick..." He imitated her pleading tone.

"Don't."

"Don't what?" He gathered her sun-warmed face in his hands, then grinned as his hat bumped her forehead. He took it off and placed it backward over Michelle's blond head. "Don't what, Mick?" he repeated softly, staring at the sweet curves of her parted mouth.

Sexual tension whispered through the heavy silence—yearning, curiosity, vulnerability. "Don't stop," Michelle whispered.

There was confusion in her eyes, as well as need. Showing what he thought was remarkable restraint, Thomas pressed the lightest, most reverent of kisses on her lips. And another... and then suddenly his plans for a gentle coercion went sadly awry. Somehow their bodies twisted together and their lips clung in a desperate embrace. White sunlight poured over them as they kissed, hot and relentless and exhilarating. Thomas felt his poor heart pounding so hard he thought it would break.

He knew he'd have to pull back soon. There they stood, in full view of the gaping tourists driving at a snail's pace along Cliff Road. The rich, they would say scornfully, the shameless rich. The setting was all wrong... but, oh, how right it felt.

And then it began to rain.

Michelle looked dazed when he pushed her gently but firmly away. Water was trickling down her face, over her clothes. The brim of the baseball cap was tilted sideways over one ear. Thomas looked at the empty blue sky before he realized the sudden cloudburst was man-made. The automatic sprinklers were on, and a damn thorough job they did.

"Timing," he muttered, holding her startled gaze, "is everything. Run."

They fled to the courtyard, Michelle tripping repeatedly over the too-long pant legs of her overalls, Thomas's baseball cap flying off her head. She was breathing hard, and it had nothing to do with the short sprint across the lawn. This was pure, unadulterated terror.

And why? Because with so little effort, he was able to make her feel abandoned, completely out of control. And *nothing* scared her like being completely out of control.

"I've lost many a woman that way," Thomas said breathlessly, shaking his damp hair out of his eyes. Something told him to tread lightly, to underplay the startling passion they ignited together. It might have been the half-wild look in her eyes, reminding him of a cornered rabbit that preferred suicide to surrender. "Oh, well, look at the bright side. You have to change your clothes now, so you may as well put on your swimming suit and come to the beach with me. Better yet, let's hop on a plane and fly to the Caribbean. There's nothing like the tropical sun if you want a great tan. How about Jamaica?"

"Hop on a plane? Jamaica?" She repeated the words as if she had never heard them before. "You're serious? You'd actually fly to the Caribbean on a whim?"

Thomas shrugged. "Who wouldn't? Have you ever been to Jamaica?"

"No, but—"

"You'd love it. It's one of those places where you never want the days to end. I spent Christmas there last year, at Port Antonio. We can go snorkeling off the coral reef, swim in the Blue Lagoon."

For a moment, she actually considered it. Jamaica—with Thomas—on impulse? No rhyme or reason to it, other than the desire for a nice tan and a dip in the Blue Lagoon. She had a niggling feeling deep inside, like a tickle, that would give way to full-fledged delight if she allowed it.

She sat down hard on a low brick planter, her fingers curled around the edge. It helped to make her world steady once more. Her mind was made up, even if her body was turning traitor. Of course there would be no weekend jaunt to a tropical island. She had Sam to think of...and the two-story colonial with the picket fence. And a dog, a really big, noisy dog that would chase the postman and bury things in the flower beds. She'd never had a pet before. She concentrated fiercely on her plans for the future, her safety net.

"Where did you go?" Thomas asked quietly. There was a softly unfocused look in her eyes that boded ill for the proposed adventure. "Penny for your thoughts? Two bits? How about a Jackson?"

"I was thinking about swings," Michelle said.

"Swings?"

"Tire swings. You know, the kind you tie up in big trees? I told Sam our house had to have a lot of trees in the backyard, so we could have tire swings."

Thomas stared at her. "I thought we were planning a weekend in the Caribbean."

"You were planning a weekend in the Caribbean. I'm planning to go house hunting."

He cupped her chin in his hand, forcing her to look up at him. His eyes searched hers intently, bright with lingering desire and what was unmistakably a flicker of anger. "You're amazing, you really are. Do you think if you just ignore what's happening between us it's going to go away?"

Michelle pulled away from his hand. "I hope so."

He stepped back then, shaking his head. "You really don't understand, do you?" he said soberly. "You're not running away from me, you're running away from yourself. How far do you think you're going to get?"

"As far as I can," she whispered. And she meant it.

He was very still for a moment. Then he said flatly, "Why?"

She looked up, her throat growing uncomfortably tight. His white shirt was still damp, clinging to the hard, well-developed muscles in his upper body. His honey-colored mane of hair was a banner in the light breeze, his eyes as bright as the blue August sky. Again a wave of pure sensuality shivered through her, and again she fought it. "This is temporary. You, me...these feelings—they're only temporary."

"*Everything* is temporary, Mick. Good things, bad things, day, night . . . everything. That doesn't mean we shouldn't enjoy what we have while we have it."

"You don't understand," she said. And she couldn't explain it to him, because none of the confusion in her mind would take shape in words. How well she knew that living for the moment was a fragile and lonely existence. And yet when she looked into the restless blue of his eyes, the painful lessons were all but forgotten.

"Stop fighting me," he said softly.

Her blond head bent and she stared at the toes of her sneakers. The fight had just about gone out of her, but she didn't want him to know that. He's completely wrong for me, she told herself. He just feels right.

His hands balled into fists at his side. She didn't look up, but she could see them out of the corner of her eye.

He's completely wrong.

He left without another word. A few minutes later Michelle heard the faint sound of an engine starting up. Shading her eyes, she spotted the red Corvette parked at the bottom of the long drive. It wasn't parked for long. It pulled onto Cliff Road in a tight, hard turn, tires spitting gravel.

Completely wrong, Michelle thought again. But she wasn't sure if she was talking about Thomas . . . or herself.

She spent the better part of the evening in her Olympic-size tub, eating mint chocolate truffles and making sculptures from musk-scented bubbles. It was the perfect place for a frank conversation with herself.

I have to be honest. I'm human, like everyone else. I'm smitten by a man who is very beautiful—more beautiful than I am, certainly—and I have a feeling the obsession will become worse before it becomes better. I should be offended by the way he looks at me and touches me, but I'm not. I like it. Is this really me?

Am I a shameless hussy?

No. A twenty-four-year-old virgin could not possibly be a shameless hussy.

She sank to her nose in bubbles, chomping down on the last truffle. Thomas had been gone for hours, yet her skin still felt tight and painfully sensitive, as if she had grown into it new and it didn't quite fit. She had always thought of herself as being tough, but now when she needed that toughness the most, she was helpless, oblivious to everything but the unrelenting need for the comfort only Thomas could give. She was desperately afraid of being hurt, but the alternative—never knowing what it would be like to set herself free, just once—was suddenly just as frightening.

She was never conscious of making the decision. She got out of the bath, pulled on her shapeless terry-cloth robe— and then her eye was caught by a midnight-blue flash in her open closet door. She took out the dress, a tiny bit of a thing made of a clingy, glittery knit that left nothing to the imagination. The shoulders were completely bare, the sleeves long and tight, the skirt short and sweet. A daring dress for a daring woman who had nothing to hide. Michelle had never worn it.

She took off her robe and dropped it on the floor.

Thomas was having a bad night; consequently his employees were having a bad night. He barked orders. He snarled. He hung over the restaurant like an ominous thunderhead. The waiters cowered, tiptoeing around the corner table where the boss sat nursing his gin and tonic. Even the customers seemed wary.

Thomas knew he was acting like a jerk. He was sorry, and he would probably give everyone a raise out of guilt when he finally got his head on straight. For now, he was miserable, and he wanted everyone else to be miserable along with him.

Five hours and thirty-one minutes since he had left Michelle, and he was missing her like crazy. He had a terrible feeling that he was going to go on missing her the rest of his life. She was a rare handful, that one. She was convinced that happiness waited just around the corner, in that damned colonial house of hers. He didn't know what else he could do to change her mind. For the first time, he considered the possibility that he wasn't going to win. It was a shock to his system. He'd never wanted anyone quite this badly before. For all his experience, no one had actually tormented him before. Well, he was tormented now. Every muscle in his body cried out for mercy. Purgatory, he decided, would have a tiny, cramped skylight that gave just a glimpse of heaven.

He ordered a second drink and began burning napkins in the glass candle holder. He made quite a little fire, drawing the startled attention of Harry the waiter. Harry didn't say anything, though. Probably he wanted to keep his job.

Halfway through his second drink he became restless. He couldn't sit still, his skin felt...itchy, like he'd used the wrong detergent on his shirt. He put out his camp fire with the gin and tonic and wandered into the billiard room. A couple of college kids were playing nine ball at the corner table. He watched them, a dark and brooding presence. They became uncomfortable and left.

He racked up the balls and chalked his cue. He would play himself, since misery loved company. It should be a hell of a friendly game.

He missed his first shot. Likewise the second. On his third shot, he scratched. He was so preoccupied with his amazing lack of coordination, he didn't hear the door softly open and close.

"Are you looking for a game?" a wonderfully familiar voice asked.

Thomas straightened slowly, his fingers closing tight around the cue stick. Mick. He blinked once, just in case she was a mirage brought on by wishful thinking and gin and tonic. She wore a stretchy knit dress that left her shoulders and her luscious long legs bare. A dozen little rings on her fingers. Dangling earrings that sparkled through her loose hair. Black ballet shoes. She did love ballet shoes.

"I'm just killing time," he said softly. "Do you play?"

She shrugged, pale hair glittering on her tanned shoulders. "It's been a while."

"I'll tell you what." He hoped she couldn't hear the tremor in his voice. It gave him away, his relief, his anticipation. "I'll spot you the eight ball."

"I don't know." A wry little smile curved her lips. "I probably wouldn't be much competition for you."

"So I'll spot you the eight ball and the break. You can't ask for more than that."

"Well…" Her voice trailed off as she slowly walked over to the rack of cue sticks on the wall. "I suppose I can handle a fair game. As long as we just play for fun."

His heartbeat was strong in his throat. "I've been cured of betting. These days I just play for the pleasure of the game."

She examined the cue sticks, running her fingers along the lacquered wood before finally choosing one. "All right. We play for—" she looked over her shoulder and met his eyes "—pleasure."

It was an evenly matched game. Neither player was concentrating well. When Thomas leaned over the mahogany table to make his shots, broad shoulders stretching the smooth white material of his shirt, softly faded denim caressing his thighs and buttocks, Michelle had to make a conscious effort to breathe. She was mesmerized by the overhead lights tangling in his hair, picking out the rainbow colors she loved. When he shifted his weight from one hip to the other, she found herself shifting her own weight along with him. Watching him filled her with a warm mist of pleasure. The looks they exchanged became heated, more lingering.

Thomas had experienced the same pleasure in her...for a short time. Eventually it became more painful than rewarding. When she lined up her shots, he took to studying the pockmarked dart board on the wall with glassy-eyed intensity. His throat was arid. His senses were filled with the musky scent of her perfume. Whether or not he looked at her, he knew the delicate plane of her shoulders, the swell of her full breasts, the fragile hollow of her spine. The yearning became like a fever, radiating deep within him.

They played as long as they could. Then suddenly they were staring at each other over the pool table, the room unbearably quiet. Thomas dropped his cue stick. Michelle gently set hers on the table. Her fingers were shaking. For a moment they were still and hesitant with each other, private. But only for a moment.

"Where do we go from here?" she whispered. Heaven help her, she really didn't know.

He smiled at her gently. "It's up to you." Then, when she remained silent, he said quietly, "I have an apartment upstairs."

So near...and yet so far. Michelle thought of wandering back through the crowded restaurant, of trailing behind Thomas up a flight of stairs while curious, knowing eyes watched. "Oh. Upstairs."

He read her mind, pointing out the stained-oak door at the far end of the room. It was nestled into dark wood paneling, and almost invisible. "That leads to a hall, which leads to the back stairway. I usually keep it locked so I don't get any wandering pool players upstairs, but for you...I'll make an exception."

You'll have to make more than one exception for me, she thought. Michelle caught a glimpse of her reflection in the long mirror behind Thomas. She looked sophisticated, composed and, yes—almost seductive. She didn't look like a virgin having an anxiety attack. Proof positive that appearances could be grossly misleading.

"I'd like to see your apartment," she said.

He held her hand the entire way. She was grateful for that, for the warm fingers that closed reassuringly around hers. She was dedicated to this night with him, desperate to have her body close to his. Still, this was so hard for her, to offer herself this way—particularly since she wasn't sure what exactly she had to offer. Only her overwhelming desire for him had brought her to this point. How was a twenty-four-year-old virgin supposed to handle a situation like this with any finesse? She felt incredibly fragile inside, caught in that vulnerable space between what she was and what she would soon become. What was she supposed to do once that apartment door closed behind them? Was she supposed to act seductive? Did she know how?

His apartment was a surprise. It wasn't the sort of place she had imagined a carefree bachelor would enjoy. No fake-fur rugs, no erotic paintings, no dramatic track lighting to enhance a romantic atmosphere. The furniture was made of bleached wicker, with comfortable forest-green cushions. A plethora of potted palms and ferns crowded the corners and windowsills, and a paddle fan turned lazy circles overhead. The mantel above the fireplace was crowded with boxing trophies.

"It's nice," she said huskily. "Those trophies . . . they're all yours?"

"They are. They're also about a hundred years old. I had a mid-life crisis a while back and brought them all out of storage so I could look at them and remember the good old days."

"The good old days?" She was surprised into a smile. "You've got to be kidding. Just how old are you, Thomas?"

"Old enough," he said.

In Michelle's experience, the best way to find out some-one's age was to insult them. "Forty-two?" she guessed.

"Thirty-four!"

"Touchy, aren't you? Why are you so sensitive about your age?"

"I'm not." He looked into her big shimmering eyes, then moved just close enough to stroke her hair slowly with his palm. "I think I'm sensitive about yours."

She stared at him curiously, then turned her head ever so slightly, pressing her lips against his wrist. "You're very special, Thomas Alexander."

His instinct was to take her into his arms. Instead he found himself pulling back, asking her if she would like a drink. She blinked and nodded and said some orange juice would be nice.

Orange juice. In the kitchen, Thomas shook his head as he poured two glasses of juice. It wasn't quite what he had meant when he'd asked her if she wanted a drink. He wished she had asked for wine, or even mineral water. But, no, she had to look at him with those big brown eyes and ask for orange juice. It unnerved him. He wasn't sure why, and he didn't want to look too closely at the possible reasons.

When he carried the glasses back to the living room, she was gone. Gone. Thomas looked around blankly for a moment, then noticed her ballet shoes on the carpet next to the sofa. His gaze swung to the far end of the hall, where a soft rectangle of light spilled from the open bedroom door. His heart contracted sharply in his chest. He set the glasses of orange juice on the coffee table, making two new water rings.

He walked slowly toward the light, all the muscles in his body feeling as if they'd coiled themselves into the part of him that wanted to find relief in her. Time and space had drifted away to the farthest recesses of his mind.

She was waiting there, as he'd known she would be. She was sitting in the center of the bed, her bare legs tucked up beneath her skirt like a child's. Her fingers picked at the quilted bedspread and her eyes were huge. "Hi, there," she said.

Thomas pushed his hands in the pockets of his jeans to hide their trembling. Despite his enthusiastically cultivated reputation, he wasn't quite as experienced as some might believe. For example, he had no experience at all with a woman like Michelle, who offered her body while something in her eyes held back. "Is this what you want, Mick?" he asked softly.

It's now or never, Michelle thought. "Yes," she whispered.

Still he hesitated. "Are you sure?"

"I'm sure, Thomas." She shivered, with anticipation, fear and, yes, frustration. How on earth did she get this thing moving? And why did Thomas choose now of all times to develop patience? "Will you just...will you please..."

He smiled then, that crooked, teasing grin that reminded her more of a teenager than a grown man. Her heart skipped into double-time. "I will please," he said softly, "with all my heart and soul."

He wanted to be gentle, but the wordless foreplay during the pool game had left him raw with wanting. He came down to her on the bed in a seizure of need, his fingers weaving themselves through her hair, holding her for his kiss. Her mouth blossomed inside of his, open and hungry. Her hands went to his shoulders, clinging there as he pressed her back against the mattress. His thigh pressed between her legs and she moaned deep in her throat.

Thomas was frantic inside, scattering her face with kisses, fingers trembling and hungry on her breasts. The clingy knit of her dress slipped easily down, baring her nearly to the waist. He pulled back fractionally, staring at her beauty and shuddering with arousal.

"Thomas?" Michelle came up for air long enough to wonder if she'd given herself away, done something wrong.

His cloudy gaze connected with hers in a shaken way, his hand moving to touch the fire colors on her cheek. He felt the heat there. He saw the need in her eyes, the drowsy light of awakened passion. "Damn but you're beautiful," he said huskily, stalling for a little time. He was too close to the edge, too soon.

"You're beautiful, too," she said, quite seriously.

He smiled and started kissing her again, loving her with his mouth and his tongue and his hands, giving her all the time he possibly could. She groaned softly, arching her back against him, her fingers restless in his hair. She was heating up like soft taffy, just as sweet, just as pliable.

"It's never been like this." His voice wasn't quite as calm as usual. While his hands roved, his head bent and he slowly suckled the tip of one creamy breast. Lightly, nipping with his teeth, making her wild.

Michelle had given up on impressing him with her technique. She just drifted along the sensual current he created, letting him do the work. Concentrating on feeling... everything.

Until his hand slipped beneath her dress, closing over her thigh. Squeezing, stroking, his fingers moving dangerously close to that secret place she wasn't quite ready for him to discover yet. Suddenly the only thing she could feel was her lack of experience.

"Thomas..." Her legs tensed, drawing together. A chill of nerves shook her from head to foot.

"What?" He could hardly answer. His throat was tight and burning. He wanted this, wanted Michelle more than he had ever wanted anything in his life. "Am I hurting you?"

"No, not—" Good grief. She'd almost said it. *Not yet.*

He lifted his head slowly, looking into the dark distress of her eyes. "Mick?"

"What?"

He took a sharp breath, his own eyes growing wide as he took in the slight trembling of her lower lip, the skin that suddenly stretched tight over her cheekbones. His blood slowed in his veins, suddenly cold and sluggish.

It was her first time.

Now he saw what it was he had missed in her expression before. Determination. Joan of Arc should have been so determined. Michelle was fiercely dedicated to spending this night with him. She was here in his arms and in his bed, which was exactly what he had wanted all along. Obviously he had done something to make her want it, too. Which made her virginal status a moot point, right?

Right?

He had no idea what gave him the strength to draw back, to gently replace the bodice of her dress with stiff fingers. This was a new game, played by a new set of rules. He only wished he knew them. He tried to think back to a time when he was as tender and untried as she was, but his mind was blank.

"I'm sorry, Mick." He pushed a damp wisp of hair from her cheek, then abruptly sat up, turning his head away from the confusion in her eyes. "This isn't the way it should happen. Not with you."

Not with you. Michelle was suddenly cold. She sat up slowly, wrapping her arms tight around her body. "What did I do?"

"Nothing. It's me. I was wrong to push you like this. I was being selfish. You need time." Was this really Thomas Murphy talking? Who would have guessed? More amazing still, he meant every word. "I don't want you to have any regrets, Mick."

Her face felt as hot as her body was cold. "I came to you."

He turned back to her then, looking deep into her eyes. More than anything in the world he wanted to hold her, to make her understand. But he didn't trust himself to touch her again. "You came because I persuaded you to. Don't you see that? You want what I made you want. This has to be right for *you*, Mick. Your first time...should be something very special. No pressure. No mistakes. A memory you can look back on for the rest of your life without any regrets.''

"My first time," she whispered. Was it that obvious?

"You can set the pace. We'll take it slow. Whatever you need.'' He was trying desperately to reassure her, but the more he talked, the more she seemed to withdraw into herself. "I'm a selfish bastard, and I apologize for putting my need ahead of yours. Nothing is worth risking your happiness.''

"Whatever I need." Michelle couldn't believe this was happening. Her emotions were at a wild fever pitch, her thoughts a painful blur. He didn't want her, then? The first time in her life that Michelle DeMara had tried to give herself to a man, and the gift was returned unopened. How funny. How really funny. All dressed up like a sacrificial virgin and no place to go. She gave a hysterical little sound that might have been a sob and might have been a giggle. She felt small and battered and utterly confused, like a survivor of a hurricane. "Do you know what I need, Thomas Murphy?"

He was hurting her. It was the one thing he'd been trying to avoid. She was so fiercely independent, so proud. Damn, all he wanted was to take care of her, but he felt so bloody inadequate. "What do you need?"

"This." She swung her arm with all the strength she could muster, her closed fist catching him square on the chin. His head snapped back and his jaw went slack as he stared at her in numbed astonishment. It wasn't much of a blow, but it was a satisfying outlet for her pent-up emotions, saving her the further embarrassment of breaking into tears. "Thank you. I feel better now."

She scrambled off the bed before he could utter a word. She paused at the doorway, looking at the tiny red knuckle marks on his chin. Her breathing came fast and without depth, and her heart thumped painfully with stress. She felt panic inside, but she wouldn't let him see it.

"A black eye last week and now this." She lifted her chin and hid her shaking hands behind her back. "It's a good thing you never turned professional."

Seven

Michelle gave herself twenty-four hours to put things in perspective, just to be sure she wouldn't do anything reckless. She told herself she ought to be grateful to Thomas Murphy. He had shown her exactly what could happen when an impulsive woman acted purely on emotion. Heartache. Embarrassment. Bruised knuckles. A lesson she would never forget. Maybe one day she would write him a thank-you note.

Sunday morning she stood in front of the mirror, looking to see if the experience of the night before had left signs on her face. Her expression was composed, her color good. Only when she looked into her dark eyes did she see the quiet desperation there. She told herself she would have felt even worse had Thomas Murphy taken her up on her oh-so-generous offer the night before. It was no consolation.

With an odd detachment she wondered how long she would go on hurting like this. A good long time, hopefully—it was exactly what she deserved. Because as she stood there, she came to a frightening realization. Last night had ended nothing. Thomas was still there, glowing like a shooting star in her imagination. His touch. His humor. The endearing way his tawny-colored hair curled around the edges of a baseball cap.

"The way his hair curls," Michelle muttered, rolling her eyes in frustration. Talk about being a glutton for punishment. She had to remember that she was a survivor. She'd made a mistake—a *big* mistake—but survivors always learned from their mistakes. They got just a little tougher, a little smarter, a little more determined. They forged ahead.

That night she went to the hospital, meeting Sam in the cafeteria for his dinner break. She was pale but determined. Forging ahead took a great deal of determination.

"I'm glad you thought of this," Sam said, tearing open a packet of sugar for his coffee. "Looking at you across the table somehow makes the cafeteria food taste better. How's the clam chowder?"

"Is that what it is? I thought it was cream of mushroom." Michelle put down her spoon, tired of playing with the lumps in her soup bowl. "Sam?"

"Yes?"

Forge ahead. "Sam, I think it's time."

He took a sip of coffee. "Time for what? Pass the cream, will you?"

She passed him the cream. "Time for us, Sam."

"You've lost me." He looked at her quizzically. "I'm sorry. It's been a long day and my mind is in low idle. Time for us to do what?"

She sighed. She had been hoping Sam would get the drift of the conversation without spelling it out. It certainly would have been easier. "You know," she said, smiling encouragingly.

"No."

All right, then. She'd spell it out. "I think it's time for us to get married. We've waited much too long already...darling."

Sam put down his coffee cup. Slowly. "We've been engaged less than three weeks...darling."

"Three of the longest weeks of my life," Michelle said quickly. "I know I said I wanted to wait, but I realize I was being foolish. Why should I wait when everything I want in life is sitting right here in front of me? Why postpone the inevitable?"

"I'm inevitable?" Sam's expression was a combination of curiosity and bemusement. "I'm not sure I want to be inevitable."

"I didn't mean inevitable, exactly. I meant...inescapable. In a nice way. Look, why wait to do the right thing, that's the way I see it."

"I see." His voice said that he didn't see at all. "So you want to set a date?"

"Yes."

"Well, that's fine. All right, set a date."

"The thirteenth."

"Fine. The thirteenth of what?"

"The thirteenth of...this week."

"What? Friday? This Friday?"

"Yes. Friday the..." She faltered briefly, realizing the dubious significance of the date she had chosen. "Friday the thirteenth."

Their gazes held for the longest time. Michelle began to get nervous. She'd never known Sam to be silent for quite so long. "You know I want you to be happy," he said finally. "Are you sure this is what you want? What about your father? He won't be back for weeks yet."

Michelle was sure. She'd thought it through calmly and carefully while she was crying her eyes out the night before. "We could elope, Sam. It would be wonderfully romantic.

Then when my father gets home, we could get married all over again, a big wedding, engraved invitations, the works."

He whistled softly, shaking his head. "You're really serious about this, aren't you? You want to elope on Friday the thirteenth?"

She nodded, searching his face anxiously.

"Wow." He swallowed hard, then bravely squared his shoulders. "If that's what you want, that's what you'll get. A romantic elopement. There won't be much of a honeymoon, since I can't get off work on such short notice—"

"We'll honeymoon the second time we get married."

"We haven't found a house yet—"

"I happen to have two dozen empty bedrooms at home." She leaned forward, taking his hand across the table. One of them had sweaty palms, she wasn't sure who. "Sam? You do want to do this, don't you? I know it was my idea to elope, but I want it to be right for both of us."

"Of course I want to do this." If his voice was a little too hearty, they both chose to ignore it. "Why postpone becoming the luckiest man on earth? Especially when it's...inevitable."

"We're going to be very happy," Michelle said. "We'll be a family, Sam."

He smiled. "Yes, we will."

"So...Friday?"

"Friday."

After much soul-searching, Thomas decided on a traditional courtship.

He had no idea how to properly "woo" a woman—there was a nice traditional word—particularly one who had so recently attempted to break his jaw. But he was determined to try. Michelle might give the impression of being a little unconventional, especially around the earlobes, but in her heart he saw a true romantic, gentle and sensitive. And she had a hell of a right hook.

He wanted her as much as ever—more, if it was possible—but on different terms. His feelings were no longer carefully segregated, physical here, emotional there. For the first time in his life, he wanted a woman spiritually as well as physically. Which gave him an enormous responsibility. Caring for someone physically was one thing, meeting their emotional needs was something else again. He was flying by the seat of his pants, so to speak, but he'd always been a quick learner. At the advanced age of thirty-four, former hell-raiser Thomas Murphy was setting out to discover the fine art of romance.

But first there was a problem of forgiveness. Michelle was terribly proud, and it couldn't have been easy for her to come to him the way she had. Thomas knew he'd confused and hurt her with his startling attack of conscience. His methods might have been clumsy, but his motivation was sincere. Somehow he needed to make her understand that.

Monday morning he went to the store and bought beige linen stationery and a black cartridge pen, then sat down in his apartment to write his first love letter in twenty years.

It didn't go well. The pen leaked if he didn't hold it just so, leaving black smears on his fingertips and black fingerprints on the stationery. The pile of crumpled paper in the wastebasket grew steadily. Everything he wrote seemed either stilted and formal, or just plain ridiculous. Eventually he decided on simplicity, with just a touch of humor.

I'll forgive you for that sucker punch . . . as long as you don't tell anyone. We need to talk. Could I interest you in a nice candlelight dinner and no dancing? I'm missing you.

He left it unsigned, which he thought was a nice romantic touch, and sent it over to Cliff Road by messenger.

His letter came back less than an hour later, delivered on a silver tray by a somber fellow wearing a chauffeur's uniform. It hadn't been opened, but it *had* been neatly ripped in half.

Obviously she needed a little more time.

He devised another plan, this time something more personal. Ever since Willie Shakespeare had penned *Romeo and Juliet*, all women had dreamed of starring in their own balcony scene. And Thomas couldn't imagine a more perfect Juliet than his emotional, innocent, headstrong love. Friday afternoon he got a haircut, threatening his barber with bodily harm if he took off more than a half inch all around. Friday night he splashed on a gallon of designer cologne and drove to the ivory tower on Cliff Road. The lady deserved romance. The lady would get romance, whether she wanted it or not.

He parked the Corvette at the bottom of the driveway, wanting his visit to be a surprise. The iron gates were swung wide, which gave him hope. Had she guessed he might be coming tonight? Five days without her had seemed like a lifetime.

There was an unfamiliar car parked in the courtyard, a Wagoneer with wooden side panels. Thomas didn't pay much attention to it. It probably belonged to the housekeeper, or that nose-in-air chauffeur. He picked up several pebbles from the flower beds in front of the house. Small and round, perfect for tossing against Juliet's window. The only problem he foresaw was identifying said window. He walked around the north side of the house, counted three floors up and . . .

And saw a burglar climbing a ladder to Juliet's window.

Thomas dropped the pebbles on the lawn and ducked behind the shrubbery. He needed to get closer. There was something about that burglar that seemed vaguely familiar.

He crept over pansies and petunias, keeping low. As he got closer, he could hear the burglar talking to himself.

"This thing feels like it's made out of matchsticks. Lord help me if a breeze comes up."

He knew that voice. Thomas popped his head over the hedge, bristling. Sam? What the hell was Sam doing climbing into Michelle's bedroom?

"Michelle?" Sam's voice went from a mutter to a shout. "Michelle! Come to the window!"

A moment later the window was pushed open and Michelle's blond head appeared. "What...*Sam?* What on earth are you doing? You're going to kill yourself!"

"You wanted a genuine elopement. I'm just trying to give you one. Would you hold the top of the ladder, please? I've never been good with heights. Thank you. Ready or not, here I come."

Elopement. Thomas sat down heavily in the flower bed. Was he hallucinating from after-shave fumes? Could he possibly have heard what he just heard? Michelle had agreed to elope? With Sam? Tonight?

"Have you got your suitcase packed?" Sam's voice.

"I'm all ready, but I'm not sure I can carry it down that ladder..."

"Now there's a silly thought. Lady, this ladder was just for effect. We're going out the front door like civilized people."

Thomas heard the window sliding closed. He sat very still, seeing nothing, and counted slowly to ten.

Why hadn't he foreseen something like this happening? He knew Mick as well as anyone. She'd been hurt, and her first instinct would be to make damn sure she didn't get hurt again. Of course she went running to Sam. An elopement seemed a little extreme but Mick never did follow the expected path. The lady needed a keeper.

She wouldn't go through with it, he told himself. Having her ears pierced three times was one thing, marrying a man on the rebound was another. She might think she was going through with it, but she wouldn't. Sooner or later—and it had better be sooner—she would realize she was making a terrible mistake. And if she did go through with it, Thomas would say good riddance and let her live the rest of her life in two-story colonial misery.

The hell he would.

He heard the front door open and close. He crept around the side of the house, watching as Sam held the car door open for Michelle. Then suddenly he remembered his own car, parked in plain sight at the end of the driveway.

He took a running shortcut across the lawn, staying in the dark shadows of the trees. There wasn't time to start his car. He put it in reverse, taking a hard left as the car rolled backward. He coasted to a halt on the soft shoulder of the road fifty yards down from the iron gates. His side was killing him from the two-minute sprint.

The Mazda cruised down the driveway and turned right. Thomas waited for a few seconds, then started his car and followed behind, keeping a discreet distance.

He wondered if she had ever been spanked.

She wasn't going to change her mind.

Michelle told herself that over and over again as they drove to the justice of the peace. She was determined. For the first time in her life, she would be part of something real and stable and lasting. Mother, Father, Dick and Jane...and Spot. Probably a collie. They would be wonderfully ordinary, the Hicks family. It was all she had ever wanted.

"Are you awake over there?" Sam asked quietly, pulling up to the curb in front of a small, split-level home. "You haven't said much."

She gave him an apologetic smile. "I'm sorry. I was just...thinking. That was very creative of you to bring the ladder."

"I didn't bring it, I stole it out of your gardener's shed." He turned off the motor, staring out the window at the darkened street. "Before we go in..."

Michelle's heart started a hard, uneven beat. "Are you having second thoughts?"

A pause. "Actually, that was the question I was going to ask you."

"I'm determined to go through with it."

He looked at her quizzically. "This isn't a root canal, heart of my heart. It's a wedding."

"I know that." She laughed nervously. Why was doing the right thing so difficult? Why was doing the wrong thing so tempting? She thought of Thomas, of his carefree charm and live-for-the-moment philosophy. He dreamed of an island where he could play his harmonica and bake in the sun like a lizard. Paradise, wrapped up in a coconut shell. Obviously he didn't require much from life to be content. Well, Mick DeMara—no, *Michelle DeMara*—was cut from different cloth. She needed a great many things in her life to guarantee her happiness. Comfortable, ordinary, everyday things that she had been starving for for as long as she could remember. And she would have them.

She looked at Sam, the gentle hazel eyes, the fine-boned, competent hands. She tried to find some sort of comfort in the knowledge that she was doing the right thing. "Forgive me," she said. "I think I'm just suffering from pre-wedding anxiety."

"You know, Michelle... you could tell me anything," he said, watching her. His eyes smiled in that quiet, gentle way he had. "Anything at all."

Michelle felt a sudden tightness in her throat and the butterflies in the pit of her stomach took flight. In all the months she had known Sam, there had never been anything they couldn't share with each other. Until now. He knew nothing of the emotional turmoil she'd been wrestling with lately. Or did he? She looked away from him helplessly. "We should go in. It's getting late."

Walking into the house was like walking into a dream. Michelle met the justice of the peace, his wife, their three children. She couldn't remember anyone's name. She focused on a glass curio cabinet in the corner of the living room, crowded with dozens of family pictures and mementos. One day, she thought. And it all begins tonight.

Before she knew it, she was standing next to Sam, holding his hand while the justice of the peace spoke of love and commitment. She tried to listen, but her attention kept wandering back to the curio cabinet like a magnet. Mother's Day cards were displayed, bronzed baby shoes, family photographs, both formal and informal. She liked the old-fashioned picture frames they used, and the little brass stands. She especially liked the quilted picture frame made of pink gingham. Homemade, obviously, and by a child's hand. It was precious. It made her want to cry.

"Michelle?" Sam said softly.

She realized with a start that everyone was looking at her. Waiting for her to say something. Sam was very still, waiting along with everyone else.

"I'm sorry," she said hoarsely. "Umm...what was the question?"

Sam was staring at their clasped hands, a strange, serious expression on his face. Then he glanced up at the justice of the peace. "Excuse us a minute, will you?"

Michelle followed Sam into the adjoining room like a sleepwalker. All her senses seemed to have short-circuited. She knew she'd done something terribly wrong, but she couldn't seem to feel bad about it. She couldn't seem to feel anything.

"That question the justice of the peace asked you," Sam said mildly. "It was one of those, 'I do' or 'I don't' things."

"Oh, Sam." It was barely a whisper. She tried to think, but nothing came beyond a numbed astonishment that she hadn't been able to take this final step.

"You know what's really strange?" Sam walked slowly over to the window, holding back a white lace curtain with one hand. "I think I would have been more surprised if you'd gone through with it."

She tried to see his expression, but his back was to her. "What do you mean?"

"I can't explain, not so that it makes any sense. I just knew it wasn't going to happen." He glanced back at her, his smile tender, whimsical, perhaps a little sad. "Michelle, we've been friends—the best of friends—since the first moment we met. Give me a little credit for understanding you. Something has changed in our relationship lately." Then before Michelle had a chance to prepare herself, "If I had to make a guess, I'd say I first noticed a difference about the same time I met Thomas Murphy in your kitchen. Remember him? Nice-looking guy, looks real cute in an apron?"

"It's not like you think." Michelle swallowed hard, looking around her as if for inspiration. "Sam, you have to understand. Thomas and I aren't...it was never...anything serious. It couldn't be, not with him." Dear heaven, she was making a mess of things. She tried again, taking a deep breath and wetting her dry lips. "What you and I have is special. It's real. It's stable."

"But it's not what you need right now, Michelle," he said. "I think you realized that tonight. And as far as Murphy goes..." He shrugged, turning back to the window. "Maybe you're right, maybe he isn't the man for you. Who knows? When you've finally worked this thing through, I'll still be around. But you do have to work it through, kiddo. You can't hide from it."

Michelle gripped the back of a Queen Anne chair, lost in her humiliation and confusion. Sam was quite right. He understood her better than she understood herself. This whirlwind elopement had been born of sheer desperation, with a little humiliation thrown in for added incentive. She hadn't been marrying Sam. She'd been running away from Thomas. It was getting to be a dangerous habit with her, leading with her heart instead of her head. "I'm sorry. I'm so sorry."

"So am I," Sam replied, a new note in his voice. He was still looking out the window, but something in his posture had changed. "I'm *really* sorry."

"Sam, what can I do to—"

"Honey, if I live through the next ten minutes, I want you to know that whatever you decide, we'll always be friends."

Michelle blinked. "What are you talking about?"

Sam glanced over his shoulder, looking not at Michelle but at the arched doorway that led to the living room. "I just saw him get out of his car. He's coming in."

Michelle's head swiveled. "What? Who?"

"Murphy. He's here. And he doesn't look happy." His eyes met Michelle's.

Thomas. Before Michelle could think, before she could react at all, she heard the front door slam. There were voices raised, one booming over the rest. A second later Thomas was standing in the archway of the dining room, murder in his silver-blue eyes.

"You," he said to Michelle in a deadly tone, "are an idiot." He turned to Sam. "And *you* are in great physical danger. Now one of you tell me if you went through with it or not."

Stress brought Michelle out of her chair. "Go home, Thomas. This has nothing to do with you."

"I have a short temper," Thomas said, still looking at Sam.

"Tell him you're still single," Sam told Michelle. "Quickly."

"I'm still single," Michelle grated out, "and stop threatening Sam or you just might get yourself hurt again!"

There was a pregnant pause. Thomas slowly walked forward to Michelle, until he was so close she could feel the heat from his body. "You're not married?"

"I said that."

"Why?"

Michelle was suddenly conscious of a brand-new emotion springing like a sea wave through her body. She stood face-to-face with Thomas, a nasty storm brewing in her eyes. "How did you know we were here?" she asked softly.

After a pause in which he examined her face, he said, "I drove over to your house tonight. When I figured out what was going on . . . I followed you."

"Why, Thomas?" she asked, opening her eyes very wide. "Oh, were you going to stop me before I made a terrible mistake? Were you going to save me from the consequences of my own folly? Were you going to come to my *rescue*?"

"Now she's cooking," Sam murmured from the window.

Thomas hadn't expected to be put on the defensive. He didn't like it, especially since he was the one who had gone through hell and back again tonight. Wasn't that enough? "This marriage isn't what you want, Mick," he said finally. "You know it and I know it."

"Really? Then what do I want?" she asked in a silky tone.

Thomas glanced at Sam. Sam shrugged as if to say, Don't ask me.

"What do I want?" Michelle repeated. "You?"

Thomas took a deep, hard breath. "Look, this isn't the place to discuss our—"

"Oh, this is a fine place," she replied with deceptive mildness. "Besides, what I have to discuss with you won't take long. I really appreciate your rushing to my rescue like this, Thomas. Heaven only knows what a poor little incompetent like me would do without a big strong man like you to guide and direct her. How on earth did I get along without you all these years?"

"Speaking of getting along," Sam said, "I think I'll go out to the living room and try to smooth things over with the justice of the peace. Maybe he hasn't called the police yet.

That would be nice." He walked out of the room with a sympathetic nod in Thomas's direction.

The strained silence that followed didn't last long.

"Sam shouldn't have to handle the explanations alone," Michelle said, "so I'll make this short. Your ego is an incredible thing, Thomas Murphy. A very large, incredible thing. I didn't ask for your intervention tonight. I didn't need it. The decision Sam and I made not to get married had absolutely nothing to do with you. And it doesn't change a damn thing between us."

Thomas hadn't been lying when he'd said he had a short temper. His hands slammed down on his hips. "If it doesn't change a damn thing," he growled, "then you must still want me, right? That's sure the way it looked to me last Saturday."

"That just goes to show you how bored I was last Saturday." But even as they were exchanging barbed insults, Michelle had the nagging suspicion that the words were just a smoke screen for the desire that still shimmered between them.

Sam poked his head around the archway and cleared his throat. "Seeing as how there's not going to be a wedding," he said, "these kind people have suggested that we leave their home as quickly as possible. I don't think they've ruled out calling the police. Michelle?"

"I'm through here." Michelle tried to brush past Thomas, but his hand snaked out and caught her arm.

"We're not through," he said flatly. "Not by a long shot."

Michelle went still, her hands curling into little, tight fists. "If you don't let me go, you're going to get yourself another black eye."

After a short pause, Thomas released her arm, a faint light of amusement coming into his blue eyes. "Whatever you say, cupcake. After all, we've got all the time in the world . . . now."

Just to aggravate him, Michelle tossed back her hair and flashed her sweetest, brightest smile. "All the time in the world just isn't going to do it, cupcake."

"You don't think so?" Thomas said softly. "You wouldn't care to make a little wager?"

Michelle turned away with a dismissive shrug. Keeping her voice as casual as she could, she said, "I don't gamble, Thomas. Not anymore."

Eight

Saturday, Sunday, Monday, Tuesday...as Thomas said, he had all the time in the world—and it was driving him crazy.

Michelle wouldn't take his calls. She wouldn't return his calls. Eventually Thomas grew tired of talking to her answering machine, to her housekeeper and to Bitsy, the friendly but bubble-headed shop assistant. He'd never handled frustration well, and his overriding impulse was to storm the castle and carry the fair lady off kicking and screaming, to hell with romance. Since that bold move would probably earn him yet another black eye, he reluctantly settled on another course of action. He'd simply bide his time until Michelle contacted *him*. She just needed a little time to sort things out, to get her priorities in order. After a day or two, she wouldn't even remember why she had been irritated with him. Women were like that. Patience, that was the ticket.

Exactly a week after Michelle's almost-wedding, patient Thomas broke out in a nasty rash. The doctor told him it was a nervous reaction. Thomas had never had a nervous reaction in his life, and it made him damn mad. Was he really that dependent on Michelle? Was he that insecure? Was he that lonely?

No way.

Driving home from the dermatologist, Thomas took an impulsive detour through a beautiful residential section of Newport. He had no idea why he was wasting time driving hither and yon on streets with ridiculous names like Harmony Lane and Serenity Drive. He was anxious to get back to Shenanigans. The latest issue of *Islands* real-estate magazine was due to be delivered in the afternoon mail. He had a feeling the beachfront property on Grand Cayman Island might have been reduced in price. If so, and the owner was still willing to carry a contract, Thomas might actually be able to swing the deal. For the first time, he could actually see his someday island on the horizon.

But he didn't rush back to Shenanigans in pursuit of his dream. Instead he followed the quiet, tree-lined streets with the silly names until a For Sale sign happened to catch his eye. The house was charming—if you liked the traditional look—a two-story colonial with a shady veranda and a double garage. Although the grounds were well-kept, Thomas could see the house was vacant. He thought all those empty windows looked . . . lonely.

He decided to get out of his car and stretch his legs. While he was at it, he circled the house, peering into the windows, trying to gauge the size of the rooms. Actually, it was even bigger than it looked from the outside, a home designed for a large family. The carpets were gray, not his favorite color. His beach cottage wouldn't have any carpets at all, just cool tile floors. You'd never worry about getting a little sand on a tile floor.

He noticed that the backyard had several tire-swing trees. He didn't care much for oak trees. They lost all their leaves in the fall, and Thomas hated all those naked branches. He preferred palms. Still, Michelle would probably love this place. It looked like her dream come true. And in this neighborhood, one of the nicest developments in pricy Newport, it probably cost twice as much as Thomas's prospective home on Grand Cayman Island.

Without asking himself why, Thomas scribbled down the telephone number on the real-estate sign.

Michelle's official vacation began the last day of August. Bitsy and two part-time salesgirls would take over at Adorn Me while she was gone. She had two full weeks, and she intended to use them wisely. She was badly in need of a rest. She hadn't been sleeping well. She'd developed a tiny little muscle tic underneath her right eye. It was almost imperceptible, but drove her crazy. She blamed it on Thomas.

He'd surprised her, giving up much easier than she had anticipated. A few phone calls—which she hadn't accepted—and then nothing. Maybe he'd moved to Jamaica or Gilligan's Island or some other sun-drenched tropical isle. She wouldn't put it past him, just to pack up and head off into the sunset. Men were like that, free spirits at heart. She'd probably get a postcard one of these days. *Getting a wonderful tan. Wish you were here, but am making do with buxom island beauties.*

She decided to leave town. She would fly to Virginia and visit restored Williamsburg, perhaps rent a car and drive to Charleston and Richmond and tour the old plantation homes. She loved the sense of history in that part of the country. She would marvel at the elegant colonial architecture and collect ideas for her own someday house. It was time to focus on possibilities again. Since the elopement fiasco, she'd been curiously apathetic about the future, which was entirely out of character. It was time to get her priorities back in order.

One week, two days and approximately eleven hours since she had last seen Thomas, she had Mr. Bruderer drive her to the airport. She was early for her flight, so she bought a couple of magazines and sat down in the lounge to read. She skimmed through *Town and Country*, usually one of her favorites, but found it difficult to concentrate. She looked at the other magazine she had picked up. *Islands*... Your Real Estate Guide.

Now why on earth had she bought that?

She began on page one. She read about untouched beaches on Eleuthera Island in the Bahamas, villas in the Virgin Islands, rustic cottages in the Florida Keys. One advertisement in particular caught her eye.

Little Cayman Hideaway: Privately owned tropical paradise is ideal for the individual who wants to get away from it all in one of the world's last unspoiled places. Spacious-view sites with virgin beaches edging blue-green sea. Fishing, diving, boating, beautiful coral reef. Paved roads, electric, private landing strip and harbor. Contact Island Sun Properties, Inc.

It sounded like something Thomas would die for. Without knowing why, Michelle folded down the corner of the page.

Her flight was called. She stuffed the magazines into her carryon satchel and turned to go to the boarding gate. Her passage was blocked by a broad-shouldered man wearing rope sandals, white pleated slacks and a yellow Panama Jack T-shirt.

"Hey, cupcake," Thomas said.

Michelle took a startled step backward, staring at the bright blue eyes that were looking her up and down in that same old sweet, sexy way. His thumbs were hooked in his pockets, feet planted slightly apart. He looked very relaxed, which was more than Michelle could say for herself. "Thomas? What are you doing here?"

"I've come to save you from the consequences of your own folly," he replied. "Don't thank me, I love to feel needed."

"How did you know where I was?"

"I asked that talkative little salesgirl at your store, the one with the marine haircut." He paused thoughtfully. "I was right, you know. She can't keep a secret."

Michelle took a deep breath, feeling the knot in her stomach push up into her throat. She was flooded with so many emotions, she could hardly distinguish one from the other. Astonishment. Confusion. Trepidation. And an unmistakable, irrational sense of relief. He looked so good to her, so achingly familiar...

"I'm going on a trip," she pronounced abruptly.

"Well..." Thomas shrugged, glancing over at the line forming at the boarding gate. "I know you're *planning* on a trip. Until you're actually on that plane, and the plane is actually in the sky...who knows? Life is full of surprises, Mick. I thought you'd realized that by now."

"I'm tired of surprises. I have to go, I'll miss my flight." But she made no attempt to push past him.

"Just give me one minute," he said quietly. All in all, he was encouraged. Mick was exhibiting less of a fighting spirit than he'd anticipated. "I need to tell you something very important."

She waited, watching him. She had hope, though she wasn't entirely sure what she was hoping for. The second call for her flight was announced over the loudspeaker.

Thomas ran a hand through his hair and smiled at the floor. "This is harder than I thought."

They stood that way for a moment, Thomas keeping a close eye on the floor, Michelle juggling her carryon bag, her purse and her airline tickets. Everything was clutched against her chest, which was probably a good thing. Otherwise Thomas would have seen her heart driving up through the thin silk of her blouse.

"You look pretty," Thomas said, looking up.

She stared at him. "Thank you. Is that what you wanted to tell me?"

"Well, no... I just thought that was kind of a different look for you, that white blouse and those silky white pants. Kind of Grace Kelly with lots of earrings." He grimaced and shook his head, his hand making one more destructive foray through his hair. "Hell, what am I saying? Grace Kelly with lots of earrings?"

Michelle had to smile. For all his experience, Thomas Murphy was just as capable of floundering as she was. She looked into his eyes and saw the same uncertainty she had, the same need, the same reluctance to put himself at risk. She was touched and surprised by the fact he didn't try to hide it, any of it.

Over the loudspeaker came the final call for boarding. "Thomas, I'm going to miss my—"

"Don't go, Mick," he said.

Just like that. Michelle stared at him with startled dark eyes. *Don't go, Mick.* It was so unexpected, so... genuine. No pretenses or games. She hardly knew how to deal with it. She was so very good at pretense, and such an amateur when it came to unvarnished emotion.

She dropped her boarding pass on the floor. She didn't do it on purpose—or so she told herself—but neither of them stooped to pick it up. They remained facing each other, eighteen inches apart and frozen in place.

"You're really something," Michelle said huskily. *Do I go or stay, go or stay...*

"I know." His smile was cocky, but his eyes still waited, uncertain.

"You should have stayed away from my wedding. It was my decision." *What am I getting into?*

"I know," he said. "I ran amuck."

"So where do I go if I don't go to Virginia? I'm on vacation."

"I'm a creative person. I'll think of something, trust me."
And then he sobered, his blue eyes filled with understanding. "Just trust me, Mick. All I want is some time with you.
Time to talk and laugh and just be with each other. That's
all."

There was ten seconds of thick silence before Michelle
said softly, "I think I'd like that."

Driving home, Thomas suddenly snapped his fingers and
said he knew the very best way to start out Michelle's vacation.

He parked the Corvette next to a fire hydrant in front of
Shenanigans, telling Michelle to wait in the car. He dashed
inside and out again in three minutes, wearing his gardenia
shirt and carrying a small leather duffle bag in his hand.
From there they drove to the market, where the Corvette was
parked in the fire lane and Michelle was again told to wait.
Thomas took a little longer this time, exactly eight minutes
before he emerged with a large paper sack in his arms. He
put the groceries behind the driver's seat—at least Michelle
assumed they were groceries, he wouldn't let her look inside—and drove to Cinderella's castle on Cliff Road. Cindy
was about to visit Thomas's someday island.

Twenty minutes later, Thomas and Michelle were wriggling their toes in the warm waters of the Caribbean while
they watched the spectacular sunset. Actually they were sitting on the edge of Michelle's swimming pool, pant legs
rolled up to their knees while they kicked their feet in the
heated water, but the sunset was indeed spectacular. Michelle was wearing a tangled necklace of brightly colored
plastic leis Thomas had produced from his duffel bag. There
was a flower nestled in the hair above her ear, a silk carnation that had, until recently, been part of a table decoration
at Shenanigans. Always happy to get into the island spirit,
Thomas had donned a battered, wide-brimmed straw hat
with a bright embroidered band.

But the fun was just beginning for the lucky lady wearing the colorful leis. Thomas had yet another wonderful surprise in his duffel bag. He reached in and brought forth his harmonica with a contagious "Now you're in for a treat" smile.

"What's that?" Michelle had to laugh, watching him carefully polish the silver instrument with his shirt.

"What do you mean, what's that?" Thomas waved the harmonica in the air in front of her nose. "This little jewel will provide the perfect background music for our stay in this tropical paradise. Remember, there aren't any stereo systems handy here. We have to provide our own entertainment."

"Can't you have a personal tape player on your island, with a few good tapes? Or maybe a battery-operated CD player—"

"Because they aren't *allowed* on my island," Thomas replied, frowning at her from beneath the shaded brim of his hat. "They would disrupt the peace and quiet. Will you get into the spirit of this thing, please? Close your eyes and feel the music while you listen to the sound of the sea."

She closed her eyes, stifling a giggle. Thomas began to play...something. It took her a while before she recognized it as the Hawaiian wedding song.

She clapped when the noise—or rather, the music—finally stopped. "That was very nice," she said, her voice quivering slightly. "I didn't know you were a musician."

"I know I'm not very good," Thomas said, pushing his hat to the back of his head. "But I'll get better. I just need a few years of practice. One day I'll be so good, just hearing me play will bring tears to your eyes. Hey, look there!" He pointed to a chaise lounge. "A whale swimming in the lagoon."

"Six whales." Michelle entered into the game with enthusiasm, counting the lounges around the pool. "Your someday island is beautiful, Thomas. Much nicer than Virginia. I'm very glad I came."

"I knew you'd like it." Thomas slipped his harmonica into the pocket of his shirt. "Of course there are a few rules here. Not many, but the ones I have are very important."

Michelle's chin took on a mischievous tilt. "Such as?"

"Well, there are some things you aren't allowed to say, like 'power lunch' or 'power suit' or 'power' anything. And you can't say silly things like 'significant other.' You can't talk about BMWs or Saabs. Yuppie is a swear word. Attorney is also a swear word." He dropped his chin and fixed her with a stern look. "Also women are never allowed to win at pool games."

"Then we'd better not *play* pool on your someday island," she said sweetly, tugging the hat down over his eyes.

They picnicked on the tropical delights Thomas had purchased at the market. Hawaiian Punch, barbecued ribs, ambrosia salad from the deli and coconut candy bars. Thomas offered to play a little after-dinner music on the harmonica—he was familiar with several songs from *South Pacific*—but the sun had long since gone down and Michelle was getting chilly. She thought it might be a good idea to walk back to the little grass shack.

For Thomas, this was the sticky part. The part where he stopped pretending that they were together forever on his someday island. The part where he left her at her door with a chaste kiss. The part when he fought with his natural instincts and won. Hopefully.

Conversation was scarce as they walked around the back of the house to the kitchen door. Thomas's heart began a slow pounding in his chest when they reached the covered porch. Suddenly the memories of the day came back to him—the way the sunset had graced her, pinking her smooth skin and settling like fire in her hair. Their shared smiles, their companionable silences. And not once had he touched her, though his entire body was aching with need. He felt as if he had waited a lifetime for her. Then again, he had.

I'll give you the time you need, he thought grimly.

He opened the back door, then stepped to the side. He decided against the chaste kiss. He knew damn well he wasn't capable of it in his current condition.

"Thank you for coming to my island," he said, striving for a lighthearted tone. "You made it complete."

Michelle looked at him in surprise. "Aren't you coming in? It's still early."

Quickly, too quickly, "It's not a good idea. Not tonight."

"Oh." She stared at him, feeling suddenly warm and confused and shy. Shy? Michelle DeMara? She raised her hand, feeling the heat in her cheek. "Well, then...thank you for everything."

His smile felt stiff, like dried mud. "You're welcome. I'll give you a call tomorrow. Maybe we could go to the beach or something. The real beach."

"That would be nice."

One minute dragged into two. Neither of them spoke, neither of them moved. The cool night air seemed to pulsate with their hectic thoughts.

Why doesn't he kiss me good-night?

I owe her this much. It's got to be right for her.

Maybe I have something in my teeth.

She's chewing on her lip. I wish she wouldn't. It drives me crazy when her lips get all red and moist like that...

I feel like I've been waiting for him all my life. Well, I have. Waiting and waiting...

I love her eyes.

No one ever made me feel like this.

I'm in trouble. I don't think I can leave, after all.

They regained the power of speech simultaneously.

"Mick?"

"Thomas?"

He took her hand in his, lacing their fingers. "Sorry. You first."

"This is hard," she croaked. "I have . . . something important to say."

He waited, holding his body very still and staring into her eyes. Those soft brown eyes that were so easy to get lost in.

"Don't go," she said softly, so softly he could barely hear.

He shut his eyes tightly, then opened them again to show her the full force of his need. He closed the distance between them, slowly so as to give her time to back away if—heaven forbid—she changed her mind. But her lips parted instinctively beneath his, warm and willing. It wasn't a desperate kiss, but one of hesitant joy, the gentle touch of two lips while hearts soared. So brief, the beginning of so much.

He lifted his head, his shaky fingers framing her face while he struggled for words. No one had ever prepared him for this feeling that flooded his heart and his mind. No one had said, Brace yourself, Murphy. One day you'll meet a woman who will stay with you like a shadow even when you're apart. She'll make you feel whole for the first time in your life. Everything will be new and precious with her. She'll help you believe in all the things you've always doubted, including yourself. If you don't blow things, she could very well be your redemption.

"I'll never hurt you," he whispered, and he knew for the first time that it was true.

She kissed him on each cheek, a benediction. Then she took his hand in hers and led him inside the darkened house. There was no awkwardness, though neither of them spoke. Electricity flowed through them, one to another, a quiet sense of anticipation in the rhythmic sound of their breathing. They felt like dear friends in a sense, pleased with their ability to make this beautiful silence together. At the same time, they were just a heartbeat away from becoming lovers, warming themselves in the increasing heat. *Their* heat. He smiled at her and her face gave off a shower of light; she could hide nothing from him. For the first time in her life, she had no need to disguise her emotions. He had overcome her deepest resistances, but her inexperience and vulnerability were no longer something weak or shameful. This time there would be no soulful regrets. She wanted the memories they could create together, and she wouldn't have them clouded with—ahem—virginal reluctance or hesitation. And so she gathered up all her tortured little thoughts, her doubts and uncertainties, and simply...let them go. Voilà. This time she knew the light in his eyes was a promise, and not an illusion. The door wouldn't slam in her face. This time, this first and unrepeatable time, felt utterly and totally right.

While Michelle cuddled against him, Thomas turned on the lights in the entry hall, looking up the long flight of stairs. He hesitated.

"What's wrong?" Michelle whispered.

"This requires tact," he said, brushing a kiss on the top of her head. "I can't very well play Rhett Butler and just grab you in my arms and carry you upstairs."

"Why not?"

And so he did. He carried her up two flights of stairs, pausing at the landings to kiss her and shift her weight in his arms. He wasn't staggering when he reached the door to her sitting room, but he was breathing hard. By the time he reached her bedroom, his legs were warning him not to try another step with his precious cargo.

He set her down—a little abruptly, but that couldn't be helped—near the door. When her hand went to the light switch, he shook his head.

"No. That would be all wrong."

Michelle was surprised, and a little amused. Thomas preferred to take off his clothes in the dark? Or was he trying to be "patient" with her again? "You don't want the light on? We'll probably fall over something. The lamp in the sitting room doesn't give much light in here."

"There are lights," he said, "and there are lights. Foolish child." Grinning, he went straight to her lingerie drawer and brought forth her plastic night-light. "Setting a mood is very important."

She snatched it out of his hands, cheeks flaming. "How did you know about this?"

"You babble when you're drunk. It's absolutely adorable." He cut short her protests with a long, lingering kiss. "You're adorable. Incredible. Delicious. Perfect."

"All that?" Michelle whispered faintly. She had forgotten the night-light in her hand. She was melting into something warm and liquid. No bones. No muscles. No resistance at all.

"Oh, that's only the beginning," he murmured, his mouth initiating a deeper demand. "You're addictive. You're beautiful. You never do what I expect. You kiss like an angel...oh, yes, that feels so good..."

Michelle pressed against him, her arms circling his waist, the night-light still in her hand, still forgotten. Every cell in her body seemed to be heightened to an unbearable sensitivity. His tongue rode liquid fire on her lips. His hand wove hungry patterns in the small of her back, then slipped lower to cup her buttocks. "I can't believe this is really happening." The words were a shaky whisper against his lips.

"Maybe it's a dream. It feels like a dream." He scattered kisses on the downy-soft curve of her neck. "Promise not to wake me up...ever."

Michelle shivered hard as he lifted a knee and pressed it between her legs. "It's no dream," she whispered hoarsely, holding on to his bright blue eyes like a lifeline.

Thomas felt as if he was standing too close to a fire. His skin was tight, burning up, feverish. Too much, too quickly. He gathered her face in his palms and rubbed his cheek slowly against hers, then stepped back. He reminded himself they had all the time in the world...for all the good it did him. He wanted her so much that his eyes hurt from just looking at her.

He took the night-light from her hand and plugged it in the socket near the door. Michelle pulled it out again and walked across the room, plugging it in the wall near the bed. A small circle of light shimmered like new snow across the ivory bedspread.

"That's better," she whispered.

The room was still, the current flowing even more strongly between them. Thomas stood in the shadows, just...watching her. Her pale hair was tangled from his fingers and her dark eyes held an excitement that sent his heart slamming against his ribs.

There were so many things he wanted to tell her, so many feelings he wanted to put into words. But it was so hard, when the core of his body had already begun its primitive, rhythmic stirring. Energy rose from his thighs and gathered in the pit of his stomach. He was walking an erotic tightrope.

Now. No more waiting.

He walked toward her, his hand going to the buttons of his shirt. He was hardly aware of working the buttons open one by one, he was so lost in her eyes. The shirt fluttered to the floor near her feet. His finger tipped up her chin, then trailed slowly down to the simple V neckline of her blouse. He bent his head, his lips brushing the hollow at the base of her neck, his fingers moving slowly from button to button. The blouse fell open and she felt the air on her heated skin.

"You're so beautiful," Thomas whispered. "You and your sweet dark eyes, and your flushed cheeks. I just want to look at you..."

Her chest was rising and falling in a gradually increasing rhythm. She felt a little shaky now, but even that quiet anxiety was intensely pleasurable. Like the shock of the cool air on her skin. Unexpected. Exquisite. And it was only the beginning. She could hardly take it all in.

The blouse slipped off her shoulders and to the floor. Michelle's naked skin under her simple silk teddy seemed incredibly sensitive to the slippery, weightless material. Her nipples hardened. Her breasts were weighted with a growing heaviness. She wondered why Thomas didn't touch her, why he just stood there and ... breathed. She ached to feel his hands on her.

Still, if the mountain wouldn't come to Muhammed ...

She placed both her palms flat on his chest, closing her eyes and concentrating on this learning experience. Her fingers moved, trailing slowly over hard planes, silken angles, muscles bunched with tension. Her thumbs brushed across his nipples, and she wondered if that felt as good to him as it did to her. Possibly, since she felt his rib cage lift sharply, like someone had burned him. She liked that feeling, knowing she could affect him that way. Perhaps enthusiasm was just as important as experience. She hoped so.

She leaned forward, trailing gentle little kisses along his collarbone, surreptitiously gazing upward to gauge his reaction. A hard color defined his cheekbones. His mouth was softly parted. His breathing seemed to have stopped altogether. Pleased to have pleased him, she grew bolder and more inventive, her tongue touching on first one nipple and then the other in a light, lacy pattern. While she ... worked ... her own breasts began to ache, wanting the same attention.

"Who's seducing who?" Thomas asked in a thick voice.

"I'm *learning* things," she said with husky satisfaction, kissing the smooth hollows between each rib. "I'm sorry, but I'm very inexperienced. I need to know ... everything."

"If you don't stop kissing me there—" he sought her cheek with a shaky hand "—you're going to learn more than you expected sooner than you wanted. A man can only take so much."

That sounded interesting. She went back to his nipples, circling them with the tip of her finger. "How much?"

"About as much as a woman can take. Would you like me to demonstrate?"

Putting her head back, she looked up into his face with heated eyes. "I wish you would. I really wish you would."

There would never be another like her. Thomas smiled, and then he laughed, taking her face in his hands and drinking her in. This was the face he would be content to look into forever. This tireless bundle of energy, this beautiful, fiery, funny lady with the siren's smile and the eyes of an innocent. No... not quite so innocent.

His hands moved lower, curving warm and hard over her bare shoulders. There was such a slight space between her body and his, and that space seemed to be glowing with heat and radiance. Holding her eyes, he brought her closer, deliberately letting her feel the signs of his arousal. It was enough to set her trembling, but instead of pulling away, she pushed herself closer, hips thrusting forward. He kissed one corner of her mouth, then the curve of her jaw, then the hollow of her throat. His smile came and went against her skin, as he alternated between joy and hunger. He could smell the sweet scent of her skin, mingled with perfume and passion. He knew every breath she took. He could hardly distinguish between her heartbeat and his own. This meant so much more to him than a promise of sexual fulfillment; for the first time in his life, he knew that he'd found someone who was necessary to him. Suddenly she was everything he'd always needed and never really had... a trusted friend, a mother, a child, a lover. Filling all the empty places inside of him, soothing him, exciting him, accepting him as he was.

Michelle murmured, a pleading sound. "Tell me," he whispered raggedly, wanting to give her some measure of the joy she was giving him. "Tell me what you want."

Wordlessly she took his hands, guiding them to her breasts. Her head fell back weakly as he lifted and kneaded the tender weight, with such softness, such gentleness, that tears came to her eyes. He was infinitely tender, and she needed that tenderness to survive the intensity of her emotions. A low gasp escaped from her throat when his mouth closed over the points of her breasts, suckling through the delicate silk teddy. The fabric became damp and he blew softly on it, sending nerve chills shooting down through her body, tugging fiercely on the sexual muscles in her abdomen. Her legs could hardly support her—she was limp and taut at the same time, full of him and yet needing so much more.

Clothes were removed, one at a time, often assisted by four shaking hands. Michelle discovered that finesse had no place in the act of making love. The eagerness, the uncertainty, the overwhelming feelings of joy and gratitude, were all a wonderful part of giving yourself to another person. Naked, she stood before him without embarrassment, smiling when he held out his arms to her. Her palms learned the slope of his shoulders, the flat plane of his stomach, the hollow of his spine, while his moved with the same hunger and amazement over her. Her belly was flat against his, her full breasts flattened against his muscular chest. Clinging, gasping, they tumbled together on the silk bedspread. Arms braced on either side of her, he whispered her name as if he loved the sound of it. He kissed her until she became feverish and restless, anxious to be touched, expecting to be led into even deeper feeling.

And then he raised his body above hers, looking down into her face with passion-bright eyes. "Sweet girl," he whispered, smoothing his hands over her hair. "How on earth did I last this long without you? I can't imagine why I haven't withered up and died by now."

"You're definitely not withered." As soon as she'd said the words, she could have bitten her tongue off. To make such an indelicate observation at a time like this was inexcusable. Her inexperience was showing . . . again. The overwhelming feeling of physical and emotional bliss was her only excuse.

But he smiled at her, and that slow, crooked grin made her feel utterly adorable. "Ma'am, you shock me."

"You shock me, too," she whispered. She arched against him, her legs twining around his. "And I like it. Do you think after all this time, I might just turn out to be over-sexed?"

"It's too early to tell," Thomas said hoarsely. "But I'm hoping for the best. Oh, Mick...I've wanted to do this for so long."

"Then why haven't you?" She wriggled under him, wanting him to come to her. Nearer...to the place where she ached for him to be. This incredible, lovely man, she thought, looking at his dark-sweet face, the powerful lines of his chest and shoulders. She drank him in with her eyes, wanting to remember.

"I was scared," he said softly. "This is all new to me."

"If you expect me to—"

"Listen to me." His head lifted. His eyes were filled with a hazy passion. "Nothing, *nothing* I have ever experienced prepared me for this. Every feeling I have takes me completely by surprise. You're a first, Michelle DeMara."

"My name's Mick," she whispered.

His smile sent her into a drowsy state of ecstasy. His weight shifted, and he was on top of her, burying his head in the arch of her neck. Loving her, holding her. And then that wasn't enough for either of them, and his hands moved between her thighs while his tongue played in and out of her mouth. "Sweet girl...I want to be gentle...to give you time..."

"I'll die if you give me more time," Michelle whispered desperately. And she would, she knew it without a doubt. Her brain was on fire with enchantment. There was an aching void growing within her, an emptiness that screamed to be filled. Her thighs tightened convulsively when he poised himself above her, but she forced herself to relax, giving herself only to feeling. She held on to his shoulders and his eyes as he entered her, her blood burning through her veins. Scalding her...

She felt pain, but it soon subsided. The pain she had expected. She didn't expect the waves of pleasure that followed when he eased himself deeper within her. No one could have described it to her, no one could have prepared her for it.

He began to move within her, slowly at first, the tension palpable in the straining muscles of his back. She rocked against him with a tentative rhythm, an inability to remain still. A waterfall of kisses and love words rained on her lips and face and hair. Her imagination was full of colors and light—starlight, moonlight, sunlight. And his eyes...always his eyes, loving her, needing her, reassuring her, pulling her further into him. He made her a part of him, and he knew all that she had ever been, all that she had ever tried to hide from herself.

The pleasure rose furiously between them like the wind before a storm, and Michelle knew she had reached a point where she was completely at his mercy. She heard herself crying his name, staring at him through pleasure tears. The pressure gathered, drawing her tighter, tighter. Fire under velvet, burning, igniting. The hectic pattern of her breathing changed abruptly as she reached a pinnacle, drifting for a timeless moment in a molten sea of gold. And then she was falling, falling into a sun shower of sparkling color, hurtling to a glorious, bright destruction...

Thomas held her in the tender protection of his arms. As he stroked her hair, he wondered if she realized how much she had changed him. There were no words to describe the peace and gratitude he felt, but he knew he had to try. She deserved...great eloquence. But while he was struggling to find the perfect thing to say, his unpredictable beloved shifted her head off his chest and smiled at him with dreamy eyes.

"So tell me," she said sleepily. "Was that as good for you as it was for me?"

Nine

—

It was morning. Thomas could see the light behind his closed eyelids. He'd been awake for some time, but he hadn't moved yet. He was making plans.

First he would sneak quietly into the bathroom and draw Michelle a bath. A bubble bath, hot and steamy and fragrant. She was bound to be sore after...everything. He wanted to care for her.

While she was soaking, he would go downstairs to the kitchen and make the most incredible breakfast. Something hearty, because she was bound to be hungry after...everything. He would bring it upstairs on a tray and have it waiting for her when she got out of the bath. With a rose on the tray. He'd have to remember to run outside and find a rose. That was a nice touch.

He wanted her to feel cherished. He'd never had anyone in his life to cherish before. When he was younger, he'd been too much of a hellion to care for anyone, and vice versa. His friends, his family, had always expected the worst from him and he'd never disappointed them. Later on, when he'd outgrown the selfishness and acquired a bit of self-confidence, he'd discovered the world was full of willing women. And although they came and went in his life, with their dark-lashed eyes and husky voices, they left curiously little impression on his soul.

Until Michelle. He'd sensed in her something of a soul mate from the beginning, a spiritual orphan who couldn't quite find her place in the world. Separate they had been drifting. Together they were whole, children again, but this time without fear. Thomas felt as though he had come home at last.

He would tell her as soon as she woke up, because women needed to hear those kinds of things. Romance was alive and well and living in the grand mansion on Cliff Road. Shakespeare would have approved.

But first, the bath. Thomas raised himself up on one elbow, blinking the sun out of his eyes. And then he blinked again, because Juliet had gone hither—or yon, or somewhere—in the night. Her side of the bed was empty.

It was difficult to provide tender and romantic moments for a missing person. Thomas climbed out of bed, stark mother naked, and went in search of her. She wasn't in the bathroom, although the mirrors were steamy. She'd already bathed, then. What a busy girl.

He was on his way to the pile of clothes on the carpet when he heard a soft knock at the bedroom door. Wishing to spare the household help from exposure to his backside, he made a dash for the bed, covering everything vital with a lavender silk sheet. Lavender had never really been his color, but one made do.

"Come in," he called breathlessly, finger-combing his hair.

Michelle peered around the edge of the door. She wore a wicked smile and an enormous yellow rose tucked in her hair.

"Are you decent?" she asked sweetly.

Thomas grinned, folding his arms across his chest. "You tell me, cupcake. Would you describe me as decent?"

"Oh, you're better than decent. You're actually quite...good."

He stuck out his lower lip and his eyes reproached. "Good? Just good?"

"Conceited man. All right, you're absolutely incredible. You should be made president of the world." She kicked the door all the way open and walked into the room. She was carrying a black lacquer tray laden with food, which wasn't surprising. Thomas had hoped to do the same for her, but she'd beaten him to the punch. What *was* a little unexpected was her outfit. She was wearing an itsy-bitsy, teeny-weeny, black-and-white leopard-print bikini. It was strapless, practically topless and nearly bottomless. The plastic leis were around her neck again, covering more skin than the scant material of her bikini.

"Oh my," he said.

She dimpled prettily, shaking back her hair. She was wearing her seashell earrings again. "Good morning to you, too. I have a treat for you. I know how you feel about your someday island, so I decided to create a little atmosphere for your breakfast. You can imagine we're having a picnic on a beautiful white sand beach."

Thomas could feel his pulse hammering at the base of his skull. He glanced down at the sheet that outlined his body with embarrassing accuracy. "It had better be a nude beach, cupcake."

"It's whatever you want it to be," she replied cheerfully, shrugging. She sat on the edge of the bed, setting the tray carefully over his lap. "It's your island. Of course, if it's a nude beach, I guess I ought to take off my—"

"It's clothing optional," Thomas said huskily. She smelled like baby shampoo, and the strands of hair tickling his cheek felt like damp silk. He reminded himself that she was new to her role as woman of the world, and no doubt a little sore in unfamiliar places. This was her very first morning after, and she deserved his sympathy and consideration.

Michelle smiled, smoothing back his tangled hair from his forehead. She wondered if she would ever again be as content as she was today, or if she would spend the rest of her life trying to recreate this moment. No, she decided, it was only going to get better. Today and tomorrow and every day after, like a beautiful dream that never ended. "I kind of like playing island with you, Thomas. It's like playing dolls when I was little, only better."

He kept his eyes at lei level. "Thank you. I think."

"Now eat your breakfast, because I went to a lot of trouble to make it authentic." She got up on her knees, pulling lids off little silver plates as she described the menu. "I cut up pineapple, which is why I have this bandage on my finger. I made these from scratch—banana nut muffins, can you believe it? I dropped a bag of flour in the kitchen and made a terrible mess, but the muffins turned out great. I already had three. And this is orange juice, freshly squeezed by my own little hand."

A scrap of leopard-print material danced before his eyes, straining against the soft weight it held. Thomas's throat was dry and he felt a familiar swelling in his loins. That was the problem with clothing-optional beaches. You couldn't hide a damn thing. "You shouldn't have gone to all this trouble," he said, adjusting the breakfast tray to give himself a little more coverage. "I'm the one who should be pampering you this morning."

She snuggled next to him on the bed, propping her chin on his shoulder and looking up at him expectantly. "Why?"

It was getting a little hard to breathe. She was stretched out on her side like a cat, a sleek, golden-skinned woman with a creamy smile that he had never seen before. A knowing smile. "Because that's the way it's done," he said hoarsely.

"That's the way what's done?"

"The morning after." He popped a piece of pineapple in his mouth and chewed fiercely. "I'm the one who is supposed to be cherishing you."

Michelle chuckled softly, rubbing the tip of her nose against his shoulder. "Well, this is my very first honest-to-goodness morning after, so you'll have to excuse me. Besides, I wanted to cherish you. I owe you a debt of gratitude."

He glanced sideways at the top of her tousled blond head. "For what, pray tell?"

"Enlightenment." She murmured the word with husky satisfaction. She pulled back and smiled at him, fascinated by the way his hair sparkled in a rainbow of sunlight around his head. The color in his lean brown face was fresh, something that on a woman would have been called a blush. "So how about if you let me do the cherishing for a while? After breakfast I'll run you a nice hot bath—we'll turn on the Jacuzzi—and I'll scrub your back like an obedient island maiden. Doesn't that sound nice?"

Thomas knew exactly what would happen if Michelle tried to cherish him in the immediate future. He would completely forget that she was sore in unfamiliar places. Rather than risk temptation, he said firmly, "We need fresh air first. And exercise."

"Last night I got plenty of exercise."

He polished off his muffin in two bites. This was no time to linger over breakfast. "First I need to drop by Shenanigans and check on things there. Then we could go to a movie or something. And tonight we'll change into fancy clothes and you can put on a great many pair of earrings and I'll take you out to dinner. I'll even pay." That was at least twelve hours of respect and consideration before they were alone again.

It all sounded like a waste of time and energy to Michelle. "Wouldn't you rather stay here? How about a sauna? We have a sauna downstairs in the basement. Doesn't that sound better than nasty old fresh air and exercise?"

Thomas dropped his head back and covered his eyes with his wrist.

"Tempting, isn't it?" she whispered.

"No." He was going to give her every ounce of consideration she deserved if it killed him. "I mean, yes, of course it's tempting, but I really need to go over to Shenanigans. Everyone there probably thinks I'm dead. And besides, I need to sign paychecks." Actually, the employees weren't due to be paid for another week, but they would probably enjoy getting their checks early. "Besides, it's a beautiful day outside. I want to enjoy it with you. We'll just be . . . mellow today, take things easy."

Michelle was disappointed, but she understood that Thomas had to look after his business. She would just have to wait until later for further . . . enlightenment.

Everything within her yearned toward him, but she had to content herself with a soft kiss at the corner of his mouth. "You're a hard man to cherish, Thomas Murphy."

"You're not so easy, yourself," he muttered, his hands working through her hair. He closed his eyes, breathing in her fragrance. How he loved the smell of this woman. His lips brushed her cheek, then inexorably lowered to her parted mouth. It was a kiss so soft, so tender, he could have floated in it all the way to heaven.

He shifted his weight on the bed, nearly sending the breakfast tray to the floor. As it was, the juice glass slid into the plate with a clatter, bringing him back to reality. He picked up the tray and held it out to her, then quickly climbed out of bed. He kept his good side to her, which at the moment, was his backside. "Thank you for the breakfast," he said, heading for the bathroom. "I'm going to take a quick shower. And you..."

Still holding the tray in her hands, she looked at his lean, powerful body with dazed longing. "Yes?"

"You stay here."

He cherished her throughout the entire day. It was the greatest test of self-control he could imagine, but he passed with flying colors.

They went to Shenanigans, where he surprised the employees with their early paychecks. They went to lunch. They went to a movie. Later on, they changed into their fancy clothes and ate their way through a seven-course meal at an exclusive restaurant on the wharf. Thomas wore his one really good suit and a noble smile. Michelle was a heartbreaker in a backless midnight-blue dress that left him gasping for air from appetizer through dessert. If he kept this cherishing business up much longer, he was apt to go crazy. Or blind.

After dinner they walked down to the beach. Michelle took her shoes off, enjoying the freedom from wobbly, four-inch high heels. She was never comfortable in high heels. As a matter of fact, she hadn't been comfortable all day long. She'd been...itchy. Lunch had been unappetizing. The movie had been dull. Even dinner had seemed tasteless. Nothing had looked or felt good to her the entire day... except for Thomas. And he seemed determined to prolong this fun-filled day to the bitter end.

For the life of her, she couldn't imagine why. If she'd had a little more experience with the principles of ravishment, she might have thrown Thomas down on the sand and had her wicked way with him. But she wasn't sure enough of herself to reveal the physical need that was growing by leaps and bounds, and heaven knew Thomas wasn't giving a darn thing away. He was a rock.

So they walked and they talked like two old friends who had just happened to run into each other.

"It was a nice dinner," Michelle said. "I really enjoyed the..." For a moment, she couldn't remember what it was she had eaten. "The crab. It was really good crab."

Thomas slowed his pace slightly, so he could see the gentle curve of Michelle's spine revealed by her dress. He was a glutton for punishment. "I'm glad you enjoyed it."

"It's been a very full day," she went on, hoping he would offer to take her home. She even yawned delicately.

Thomas barely heard her. He was preoccupied with her walk. Her hips were swaying quite naturally, and she moved with graceful, even steps. Wouldn't she be walking funny if she was still...sore? How long did it take women to feel more like themselves again? "Would you like to go somewhere for a drink?"

"No." Michelle flushed, hearing the desperation in her voice. "No," she said more calmly. "This is very nice here. Just walking and talking with you." Silence. Silence. Why did he keep dropping behind her like that? What was he looking at? "I like to feel the sand between my toes. Going barefoot has to be the best feeling in the world."

"Not quite." He sighed, digging his hands in his pockets and trudging on.

"What did you say?"

"I said it's a beautiful night."

They continued their walk in strained silence. Suddenly Michelle stopped dead in her tracks. "Thomas?"

"What?" He watched her warily. She had a look about her he hadn't seen before.

"I have something very important to say." She frowned, trying to find the words that would articulate her need without sounding desperate. "Please don't think I haven't enjoyed our day together, but...I'm twenty-four years old, Thomas. Last night I found out there really is a Santa Claus. I have a lot of Christmases to make up for."

Thomas stood very still. "That was a beautiful speech," he said. "And I have a lot of Christmases to make up for, too."

"Can we go back to the car, then?"

"Let's run," he said.

He got a speeding ticket driving home. He couldn't quit laughing and the officer asked if he had been drinking. Thomas denied it, but the policeman still insisted that Michelle take over the wheel.

Back at the house, she spent ten minutes going from room to room to room, turning on all the lights. Every single light in the house, from the basement to the fourth floor. The mansion on Cliff Road looked like a giant Christmas tree.

Thomas followed her, laughing and dragging her close for kisses, feeling as if he was caught in the tail of a hurricane. She wanted light, she would have light. And music. She went to the kitchen and pressed buttons on the central intercom system. She found her favorite station, rhythm and blues. Billie Holliday's rich, sad crooning filled forty rooms.

"Now we can decide," she said, holding Thomas's hand and running up the stairs.

"Decide what?" Thomas pinned her against the wall on the third-floor landing. "How to begin? I could suggest—"

"Not how. I know how, thanks to you. Where."

She decided on the bathtub. She told Thomas to sit on the bed, not to move a muscle until she got back. He informed her there were certain muscles he had no control over.

In the bathroom, Michelle turned on the water, steaming hot, then poured in a handful of musk-scented bath crystals. Considering the size of the tub, she knew it would take at least twenty minutes to fill. That gave her plenty of time.

Thomas was where she had left him, loosening the knot in his tie.

"You started without me," she said in a wounded voice.

"Sorry." He tucked his hand in his lap and gazed at her expectantly. "Well? What are you waiting for? Come and ravish me, cupcake."

Watching him, Michelle caught a sparkle of amusement in his eyes. "What's so funny? You don't think I'm capable of taking the initiative?"

"Angel, you could initiate me up one side and down the other. It's all a question of inhibitions."

"You think I'm inhibited? *Me?* I'll show you inhibited, Thomas Murphy." Desire and frustration sent an avalanche of need through her. Catching Thomas off guard, she tumbled him on his back, covering his face and neck with hungry kisses. Fervent sensations filled her mind, the scent of his cologne, the damp satin of his lips. She kissed him everywhere she could reach, her hands playing in his glossy hair. She pushed at his jacket, hungry to feel his skin. The buttons on his shirt were irritating. She finally ripped the last one off. She watched it pop into the air and could hardly believe Michelle DeMara was literally tearing a man's clothes off.

Thomas was tugging at her zipper. She stood, slipping out of the dress in one fluid movement. She wore absolutely nothing underneath but a pair of lace panties. She grinned at the dazed expression on her lover's face. She could get used to this shameless behavior.

She heard his involuntary exclamation as she bent to him, the lace panties flying in the same direction as the button. She worked at his pants with less expertise than enthusiasm. It seemed like forever to her before they were fully together, skin to skin, the heat rising between them. Between the drugged, open kisses they shared, she whispered, "How am I...doing so far?"

"Not bad for a beginner." He rolled suddenly, pinning her beneath him. His fingers threaded through hers and he lifted her hands above her head, holding them there against the tumbled pillows. She squirmed. "But now it's my turn."

She gasped as his mouth went to her breasts, suckling, licking, biting lightly. She could feel a sharp, dull ache begin low in her. "Oh, Thomas...I need..."

"I need, too, Mick." His words were ragged, the breathless tone exciting her. His mouth went lower, touching her on her stomach, his tongue tracing circles of flame. And then lower, discovering her, setting her on fire, until Michelle was as frenzied as a whirlwind. Her hands were free now. She tangled her fingers into his hair, working them in and out, trying to hold on to something, trying to keep herself sane. Her breath came in shocks and her head moved from side to side. He was telling her she was beautiful in elated, half-formed words, again and again, but she could hardly hear him over the beating of her own heart. His fingers replaced his mouth on her, making her wild. He caressed her until she felt nothing but a burning need, and she cried out, "Please, Thomas...please..."

And then he was above her, filling her eyes and her heart and her body. Desire had stained his face with heat colors and his eyes were darker than she'd ever seen them. Something about the tension in his face told her he was holding back, and impatiently she thrust her hips against his. She didn't want gentleness. Not now.

He seemed to lose his last vestige of self-control. He thrust into her again and again. They were one, joined in a shock of movement and pulsation. Clinging to each other, desperate for something that might have been death and might have been birth.

There were no more words, but Thomas heard a cry of such longing from Michelle that it would echo in his dreams forever. Was this love? He couldn't imagine what love could possibly add to the intensity of this experience. And then the storm broke within him, and he felt as if every cell in his body would burst from the ecstasy. And when that sweet release came for her, the fever pitch of her emotion causing her to weep in his arms, he finally knew what it was to truly cherish.

"Mick?"

"Hmm?"

"Sweetheart . . . wake up."

"I will . . . in the morning . . ."

"Listen . . . do you hear that?"

"What?"

"I think I hear water running."

They dedicated Sunday to love, and neither of them realized that the sky drizzled rain from dawn till dark. Thomas gathered memories in his mind like a scrapbook from a weekend vacation: Michelle dressed in his shirt and a scowl, mopping up water in the bathroom; Michelle lying on her back in the sauna, her body glistening with perspiration; Michelle squealing and sliding backward down the oak banister and into Thomas's arms. So much love and laughter, more than he knew in a lifetime.

They were rudely interrupted by the ordinary and mundane on Monday morning. Thomas had to work and he had a dentist appointment scheduled for the afternoon. Michelle had her accounting class Monday night. Thomas offered to drive her to the class, but Michelle refused. She preferred to have her own car at the college, since she never knew when class would let out. Thomas offered to attend the class with her and she laughed and pushed him out the door. She didn't realize he was serious.

By nine o'clock that night, however, she wished she had taken him up on his offer. The professor had turned over the entire class period to a guest lecturer from the IRS. Michelle swore the man didn't speak English, she was so bewildered by the technical terms he used. She listened for the first half hour, dozed through the second, and was considering sneaking out of the room for a candy bar from the vending machine when a new student walked through the door and brought her sleepy senses to life.

A very good-looking student, with longish honey-colored hair and sparkling blue eyes. He shut the door a little too hard and a painting of the college president fell off the wall with a resounding clatter. Fortunately the picture wasn't framed beneath glass. Muttering an apology, the new student replaced the picture, then found a seat directly behind Michelle. Every female in the room sat a little straighter—with the exception of one. Michelle slumped downward in her seat, her face buried in her hands, her shoulders quivering.

"Excuse me," Thomas whispered, poking her in the back. "I forgot my pencil. Do you have one I could use?"

Still shaking with laughter, she passed a pencil over her shoulder. Quiet was restored and the lecture began again. Michelle stared straight ahead, determined to endure, but it was impossible to concentrate. She felt Thomas's every movement, every sigh. And there were plenty of sighs as the speaker droned on in his nasal monotone.

Ten minutes later she felt another tap on her shoulder. Thomas passed her a folded piece of paper with her name written on the front. She started to giggle again, quickly disguising the sound with a little cough.

Dear Mick—this teacher is so boring. I think he's a weanie. Can you come to my house after school and play? Love, Tommy.

She waited a few moments, then wrote her answer on the back of Tommy's note.

Dear Tommy—yes, I can come to your house and play. What do you want to play? XXXOOO, Mick.

Her answer came sailing back on a piece of paper folded like an airplane.

Dear Mick—I want to play house or doctor. Love, Tommy.

Michelle didn't trust herself to pass any more notes. Her face was red and her eyes were watering. She had the hiccups from stifling her laughter. She leaned forward in her seat, hoping Thomas would get the message and leave her alone for the remainder of the class. And he did, for about two minutes. Then she felt his knee rubbing against her bottom with a gentle, almost imperceptible pressure. Tingling, distracting. She scooted forward in her chair to escape him. She had peace for another ten minutes.

She decided it would be a good idea to leave class early. She gathered up her papers and books and walked out, glaring at the new kid as she passed him. He smiled sweetly.

He caught up with her as she was putting on her sweater in the hallway. "Hey, Mick! Wait up. You forgot your pencil." He nestled it into her hair above her ear. "Thanks.

Next time I'll bring my own. Hell, next time I'll bring my Walkman so I'll have something to listen to."

"There won't be a next time." Michelle tried to sound firm, but it was impossible when he looked at her with that boyish smile that claimed to know everything about everything. "Matter of fact, they probably won't let *me* in next time."

"Then you ought to be grateful," he said solemnly. "That was the most boring thing I've ever endured in my life. More boring than my dentist appointments, even."

"Necessary, though," she said. "Seeing as how I own my own business and I can't even figure out self-employment tax."

"So we hire an accountant. You'd never have to worry about doing the taxes again, you wouldn't have to attend this disgusting class and you'd have more time to be with me. What could be better?"

She smiled sweetly. "Learning to do it myself."

"That's illogical."

"That's immaterial."

"You don't have to do everything yourself."

"What if you want it done right?"

"But you just said you can't do it right."

"That's why I take disgusting classes, which puts us right back where we started."

He looked at her blankly. "I think the dentist gave me too much Novocain today. You're beginning to make sense."

Michelle shrugged and smiled and started to walk.

Thomas moved in close behind her, digging his hands into the back pockets of her jeans. When he spoke, his voice was an ingenious, husky whisper against her ear. "So, Mick . . . do you wanna go out in the car and neck?"

She shivered, feeling a tingle of anticipation. "Maaaybe," she drawled childishly.

"You wanna go to my house and play?"

"I guess so." Still the hesitant little girl.

"You wanna have a slumber party?"

She laughed, every inch a woman. "I'd love to have a slumber party, Tommy."

Ten

Thomas had never experienced so much joy as he did in the days and nights that followed. He discovered in himself an ability to enjoy the smallest, most inconsequential things. The way Michelle's body curved like a spoon against his at night, her arm over his waist. Or waking from a deep sleep and finding her stretched out on her side, just watching him. Kissing her in the soft first light of morning, when the sleep was still in her eyes and in her voice. The way she pursed her lips and blew her bangs away from her eyes when she was frustrated. The hiccups that came when she laughed too hard. The fourteen days of Christmas.

Before he knew it, Michelle's vacation was over and she went back to work at the boutique. Most nights she didn't get home until after nine, which was a nasty adjustment for Thomas. He was used to monopolizing her evenings. Shenanigans only took up so much of his time, and he'd always had a low threshold of boredom. Which was probably the reason he telephoned Constance Lipman.

Constance Lipman was thrilled to receive his call. She arranged to meet him at six o'clock that evening, promising him that he was in for a treat.

Driving to his appointment with Constance, Thomas asked himself over and over what on earth he was doing. He didn't want to meet this woman. He didn't want to lead her on. No, this was definitely a mistake. He'd just tell Constance he'd changed his mind, and apologize for the inconvenience.

But Constance was waiting for him in front of the two-story colonial on Harmony Drive with listing book in hand. She was a stocky woman with silver hair and formidable shoulders. She descended on him before he was halfway out of his car, shaking his hand with the force of a jackhammer. "You must be Thomas Murphy. I'm Constance Lipman from Dean Beck Realty. A pleasure to meet you."

"Actually, I find I don't have a great deal of time this evening—"

"Then we'll get a move on," she said briskly, motioning him through the front gate. "This is a dream house, Mr. Murphy. Truly a family home, designed for comfort and livability. Mind the garden hose, I wouldn't want you to trip."

Thomas decided it might be simpler just to tour the home, rather than to try and escape Constance Lipman. He followed her from room to room, nodding his head in all the right places as she extolled the virtues of this particular home in this particular neighborhood.

"The kitchen is a delight, Mr. Murphy. I can promise you your wife will love it. There's something about a fireplace in the kitchen that makes it so homey, don't you think? You'll notice that there is also a formal dining room, which is so convenient for entertaining company. And if you'll follow me this way, you'll see the master bedroom suite is located on the main floor, while the children's bedrooms are all on the second floor. That guarantees a certain amount of privacy, which most parents truly appreciate. Do you have children, Mr. Murphy?''

"No,'' Thomas said, wondering if he should also confess he had no wife.

"Well, this is certainly the home to consider if you're thinking of having children. Can't you just see this beautiful home decorated for Christmas? All the little stockings hanging in a row on the fireplace mantel in the living room, a Christmas tree in front of that lovely bay window . . . well, what could be nicer? Would you like to see the garage?''

But Thomas had had quite enough. He thanked Constance for her time, and promised to call her after he talked to his "wife.'' He was out of that house in the space of three heartbeats, and he felt like a man who had just made a narrow escape. What on earth had he been thinking of? This wasn't what he wanted. A thirty-year mortgage? Leaky pipes? Gray carpets? Siding that needed painting every year? *Six bedrooms?*

He was supposed to meet Michelle at Adorn Me for a late supper. On the way to the boutique, he stopped by a travel agency and picked up a dozen brochures on the Hawaiian islands. He'd never considered Hawaii as a possibility for his someday island; it was too commercial for his taste. But it was a beautiful place to vacation and Michelle would probably love it. Besides, Thomas felt like he needed a vacation right about now.

Zipping along the coast road toward Michelle's store, Thomas threw Constance Lipman's business card out the window.

Michelle put the Closed sign in the window a half hour early that night. Business was slow, and she'd had a raging headache all day. She needed to take care of the paperwork so she could go home and crawl into bed. She'd never felt so exhausted in her entire life.

She'd completely forgotten Thomas was picking her up for dinner until he walked into her office.

"Hey, brown eyes," he said. "I saw the Closed sign in the window. I thought you were open till nine."

"I closed early." The throbbing in Michelle's head was like a furnace, and the room seemed stiflingly hot, as well. "Business was slow tonight. Besides, I'm so tired I can't think straight."

Thomas grinned and walked behind her chair, massaging the tight muscles of her neck. "Poor cupcake. Have our little slumber parties been wearing you out?"

"Guess so." She closed her eyes and rested her forehead in her hands. "I just want to get my work done and go home. Do you think we could go out to dinner another night?"

"On one condition," Thomas said. "I get to choose the restaurant."

"Fine." Rather than relaxing, her muscles seemed to be slowly hardening, like concrete. "Anywhere is fine."

"Okay. I'll make reservations at the Black Pearl for next Friday."

He was being so understanding. "Good. I'll look forward to it."

"You'll have to pack a bag," Thomas added almost incidentally. "The Black Pearl is in Hawaii, on Maui. I thought we'd spend a long weekend there. We can leave next Thursday and come home next Tuesday."

Michelle could hardly hear him, hardly knew what he was saying. She tried sluggishly to concentrate. "What are you talking about?"

"I'm talking about Hawaii." He pulled the brochures from his pocket and dropped them on her desk. "I have an urge to take you away from it all. We need a vacation."

"I just had a vacation," she said, twisting a neck that had no flexibility left in it to look at him. "You know that. I've only been back at work three days."

"You're the boss, you can leave things in Bitsy's incompetent hands for a few more days. Come on, it'll be fun. No responsibilities, no pressure, no appointments to keep or make or break. Five days of pure unadulterated fun."

"I can't just pack and fly off to Hawaii!" She stared at him incredulously. He was sounding like a man who desperately needed a break from his everyday grind. Which was puzzling, since he'd claimed to be happier in the past two weeks than he'd ever been in his life. "Besides, what about Shenanigans?"

"Shenanigans will survive without me for a few days." Underneath his bright good humor, Thomas had a sneaking suspicion he was acting completely irrational. He had no idea what was driving him to push for this spur-of-the-moment getaway. "Come on, just throw caution to the winds and say you'll go. Who knows? You might discover that island fever is catching."

"I have a job. I have responsibilities." For the first time, it occurred to Michelle that she wasn't tired—she was sick. Couldn't he see that she wasn't well?

"We both have responsibilities." He sat on the edge of her desk, picking up one of the brochures and staring at it thoughtfully. "Since when does that mean we can't have a good time?"

"I'm not stopping you from having a good time!" She was dangerously close to tears now. When she felt better, when she could think clearly. Then she would understand his sudden urge to get away from it all. As it was, she couldn't quite shake the feeling that perhaps she might be one of the things he wanted to get away from.

"I don't get it," Thomas said flatly. "All I want to do is be with you."

"We can be together here."

"And we can be together in Hawaii. Doesn't sound like much of a choice to me, Mick."

She stood slowly, focusing on the Pearl Harbor brochure on her desk until the room stopped spinning. "Look I'm exhausted. I'm going home. Let me know if you fly the friendly skies, won't you?"

Thomas was mad. He was mad at Michelle for acting like a mature and responsible adult. He was mad at Constance Lipman for being so damned enthusiastic about the two-story colonial. Most of all he was mad at himself, because he was allowing a startling and unexpected show of domesticity to throw him into a panic. So what if he had made an appointment with a real-estate agent to look at a house he didn't want for a wife he didn't have? It wasn't like he'd *signed* anything.

"I guess I got a little carried away," he said. He felt like a fool. He wanted to explain to her about the house and Constance Lipman and his panic attack, but he couldn't. It was one of those situations where you were damned if you did and damned if you didn't. "I'm sorry. It was a crazy idea, just asking you to leave like that."

"That doesn't mean you can't go," Michelle said softly. She felt like yelling, but it would have hurt her poor aching head. She leaned both hands on her desk for support, feeling like something inside her was breaking apart. "You're a free man, Thomas. If you want to go, go. Hawaii, Fiji, Jamaica, Puerto Rico...pick an island, any island."

"Look, we'll just forget the whole thing, all right? It's no big deal."

"That's your problem, Thomas," she said, staring at him through a fever haze. "*Everything* is no big deal. It's all just . . . cake."

"Cake? What the hell do you mean, cake? That's the stupidest—"

"I'm going home." She grabbed her purse and walked out of the store. She didn't think about turning out the lights or locking the door. Thinking, like talking and walking and breathing, hurt. The night had grown chilly, but the air around her still seemed to steam.

Thomas caught up with her as he was climbing in her car. "Wait a minute! Will you wait just a damn minute? What about the store? You left it open."

"You take care of it," she mumbled, rolling up her window and locking her door against him. He pounded on the window with his fist, and the noise bounded through her head like a swelling sun. She would have liked to give him another black eye, she really would. Sobs began to burn in her aching throat.

The key wouldn't fit into the ignition, until she figured out she was using her house key. When she finally got the engine started she was crying like a baby, superheated tears that dripped off her nose and chin. She couldn't see a thing, not a darn thing.

She turned on the windshield wipers. It seemed logical.

She had no idea how she found her way home. Her fever skyrocketed, and traffic lights became more decorative than necessary. Strobe lights in red, yellow and green.

Pulling into the courtyard at home, she hit the brake instead of the gas and ended up parking the Mazda in a flower bed. She didn't care. She was enormously relieved to be alive, and no longer behind the wheel. She cried with the relief, all the way to her room.

She slept, still in her clothes. She returned to awareness in the middle of the night, shaking from cold and fever and frightened of the dark. It took her forever to find her night-light, and longer still to plug it in. The wall sockets were moving constantly. Then she wrapped herself in her bed-spread like a cocoon, trying to ease the icy chills that rattled through her muscles. There seemed to be a north wind whistling through her room. She heard her own voice crying weakly for Thomas. And then she cried again, because he had wanted to leave her and go to Hawaii and she had left her store unlocked and she had hurt Sam's feelings and Thomas had never said I love you. So many things to cry about.

She had no idea how much time passed. Sometimes the room was light, sometimes dark. The night-light burned on. She went to the bathroom when she was thirsty and drank from the tap, splashing water on her dry, heated skin. The phone rang once, but she was delirious with fever and knocked it off the night table. She couldn't manage to free herself of the snarled bedcovers to pick it up again.

Sleep became a half-waking blur of dreams and nightmaress. One night she dreamed that Thomas was with her, sponging her face with cool water and whispering in gentle tones. She woke crying, because she wanted him so badly. It took her a long, shuddering moment to realize he was really there, touching her, talking to her. Or was he? She didn't know if he was real or a trick of the fever.

She touched the shadowy face above her with a trembling hand. "Are you really here?" The words were clear but hoarse.

"Where else would I be?" he said softly. "No, lie still. We need to get your fever down. Close your eyes. Rest."

She fell asleep again almost immediately. In her dreams she felt his hand on her forehead, and the cool cloth pressed again and again on her cheeks, her neck, her chest. Gradually her restless mind stilled, and she found her first peaceful sleep in days.

When she opened her eyes again, the room was full of light. Thomas was gone. The wet cloth and the bowl of water on the night table told her she hadn't dreamed him.

She realized she was wearing her pink velour robe. She couldn't remember changing her clothes. The belt had somehow become tangled around her wrist, and she was trying weakly to free herself when Thomas walked through the door.

Michelle had no idea what she must look like. But never had she seen Thomas look so...haggard. His face was shadowed with brown stubble, and his eyes were underlined with dark circles. His shirt was unbuttoned and hanging outside of his jeans, the sleeves rolled to the elbow. One side of the collar was up, the other down.

"I thought you'd gone," she whispered, wetting her cracked lips with the tip of her tongue. "You look awful."

Thomas stared at her, trying to decide if she was finally lucid or tiptoeing through the tulips again. "You look pretty awful yourself," he said. "How are you?"

"This robe has me," she said weakly, feeling idiot tears burn her eyes. "I'm all tangled up in it."

Thomas took a deep breath, and it felt like the first one he had allowed himself for the past two days. He'd called his doctor—several times, actually—and was told Michelle probably had the flu virus that was going around. She would be fine in a few days. Still, Thomas hadn't been reassured. She'd seemed so fragile when he'd held her in his arms, and the heat of her body had been scorching. But her eyes seemed to have lost their fever brightness and she'd managed to put an entire sentence together that made sense. Obviously she was on the mend, just as the doctor had promised. Repeatedly.

"Here, let me." He went to her, slipping the tangled belt off her wrist. "There. Why are you crying?"

"I don't know." She stared at him through a watery screen. "I think I'm thirsty."

A smile entered his tired eyes as he felt her forehead with his palm. It was cool. "That sounds like a good reason to cry. I'll go get you some juice. Does that sound good? I'll be right back."

"Yes. No, wait." She slashed at her tears, not at all sure where they were coming from. "What day is it? How long have you been here?"

"It's..." He frowned for a second, trying to remember. "Friday. I've been here since Wednesday night."

"Did I call you?" She vaguely remembered trying to pick up the phone.

"No," he said quietly. She hadn't called him. It was something Thomas was finding very hard to live with. "I tried calling you all day Wednesday, but the line was always busy. I got worried and came over late that night."

"How did you get in?"

His smile twisted. "You left the front door unlocked, what else?"

"What about the store, who's—"

"Don't worry. Bitsy's handling things. Here." He pushed the damp washcloth into her hands. "Hold this against your eyes. I'll be right back with your juice."

She must have fallen asleep again before he was out of the room. She blinked, and he stood before her with a glass of orange juice in his hand. She tried to sit up, but she hadn't the strength. He supported her in his arms, holding the glass for her to drink. She took a sip or two, then pushed it away.

"You're cranky when you're sick," Thomas observed mildly.

"I'm not sure it's going to stay down." She shivered, her hands pulling at the covers. "It's cold in here, don't you think?"

Thomas sat on the edge of the bed, nestling her limp body against him. "There," he whispered. He could see her eyelids growing heavy again. "Is that better?"

"Yes. You're warm. Thomas?"

"What?"

"Thank you for being here."

His arm tightened around her, his chin resting against the top of her head. "That's where you're all turned around in your head, lady. You don't need to thank me for being here for you. I want to take care of you." He brushed his lips lightly across her forehead. He suddenly realised how tired he was. He hadn't slept for nearly forty-eight hours. He closed his stinging eyes to rest them. "Lie still, Mick. I'll be right here."

And they slept.

He stayed with her until Sunday. She was still weak, but she was sleeping and eating well. He could sense the moment she began feeling self-conscious about depending on him. She started pushing herself, going up and down the stairs, washing dishes, doing the things she wasn't ready to do yet. Thomas knew she was at the point where she would get more rest if he left her alone.

And so on Sunday evening he came to her room wearing a prearranged smile. "I guess I'll be running along now. Harry's been managing Shenanigans while I've been staying here. I think it's time to go back home and pick up the pieces."

Michelle sat up in bed, the magazine she had been reading dropping to the floor. "You're leaving?"

He shrugged. "Isn't that what you want? You've been restless all day. I figured the situation—having me here—was making you ... uncomfortable."

He was right. Michelle had been uncomfortable, but not for the reasons he imagined. She couldn't believe how much she had come to depend on him in the past four days. This was a new vulnerability, far different, and in a way, far more dangerous than loving him physically. Because she truly didn't know if he was prepared for a deeper commitment. The night he'd come to Adorn Me and announced the Hawaiian getaway, she had sensed his restlessness. Besides, he still hadn't said the words yet...I love you. And so she held her own feelings back, her own love seeming like an impossibly heavy weight.

She gave him a smile that didn't reach her eyes and said, "Restless is a kind word for cranky. I know I haven't been the easiest patient."

"Oh, I don't know. You were nice enough to eat Murphy's famous cheese omelet three days in a row. I'll bet you're glad your housekeeper is coming back tomorrow."

"I guess we both are," she said softly.

They both lost their smiles in uncomfortable stages. Finally Thomas walked to the bed and kissed her cool brow. "Take care," he said. She was wearing a ruffled blue fleece nightgown that made her look so young and fragile it wrung his heart. "Don't push yourself, Mick. Just take it easy, and in a few days you'll be doing cartwheels again."

"I never could before." There was an uncertain pause, then Michelle added quietly, "I don't know how I can ever thank you for everything you've done."

He turned away. "Just get well."

"Let me walk you to the—"

"As you were," Thomas said in a tone that brooked no argument. "I can see myself out. I'll call you later." He stopped in front of her dresser, pulling the famous night-light out of the top drawer. He smiled faintly and tossed it to her. "You'll need this tonight."

But it wasn't until he was outside that he finally said the words. "I love you, Michelle DeMara. How I love you."

Eleven

"Well, I guess that takes care of everything." Constance Lipman stood on the front porch of the two-story colonial on Harmony Drive, a successful real-estate agent's smile on her face. "You've signed your life away, so to speak."

The woman did have a way with words. "I suppose I have."

"I couldn't help but notice...your hand shook a little when you put your John Hancock on those mortgage papers."

"A little," Thomas said. He could admit it now, because the papers were signed and his momentary panic—a nasty moment, that—was gone. As a matter of fact, he felt incredibly clever and very lucky.

He bid farewell to Constance Lipman, waving goodbye as he stood on his sidewalk in his yard in front of his home.

He was a *homeowner*. He had a lawn to mow and fertilize and worry over. He had a front porch to sit on while he read the evening paper. He had a family room with ample space for a pool table. He had an attic and a basement and a garage with an automatic door opener.

He had *six bedrooms*.

There was no time to waste. This wasn't a home meant for a bachelor with tootsie frostbite. This was a family home. And more than anything in the world, more than his some-day island or his beach cottage or his yen for adventure—Thomas Murphy wanted to make a home with the woman he loved. He wanted to make a loving and supportive family with her, something neither of them had ever really had. His little boys would play baseball and soccer and football, and have a hell of a left hook, just like their old man. And his little girls... they would have triple-pierced ears and Bambi-brown eyes, and a hell of a right hook, just like their mother. And they would all be able to play pool, though none of them would ever be able to beat their dad. Only Michelle would be allowed to do that.

He knew now that he'd never really wanted anything else. His restlessness had been nothing more than a search for meaning in his life. Paradise wasn't waiting on a sun-filled tropical island. It was much, much closer than that. What was the old saying about not being able to see the forest for the palm trees?

He didn't have a phone yet in his brand-new house. He drove to the convenience store four blocks away and called Michelle at Adorn Me. Yes, he knew it was her first day back at work, but he really needed to see her. Yes, he knew she had responsibilities, but this wouldn't take long. No, it wasn't really an emergency, but... well, actually it was an emergency. It was a terrible emergency. Could she please come right away?

He gave her the address on Harmony Drive and hung up before she could ask any more questions. And then he drove back to his house and sat on his front porch and pulled his harmonica out of his pocket.

She couldn't take her eyes off him.

There he sat, on the front porch of the most beautiful two-story colonial Michelle had ever seen, playing his harmonica. And he looked very much at home.

Michelle pulled the Mazda over to the curb and turned off the engine. And then she got out of the car, hesitating in front of the white picket fence.

"Don't just stand there," Thomas said, putting his harmonica back in his pocket. "C'mere."

Michelle watched warily as he walked down the steps to meet her. "Where are we?"

"We are at 1225 Harmony Drive." He thought she looked beautiful, absolutely beautiful. She was wearing his favorite seashell earrings and a white linen dress scooped low in the front. And white ballet shoes. Impulsively he kissed her, long and hard.

"What was that for?" Michelle asked, gasping for air.

"That was because you wear ballet shoes," Thomas said, urging her up the front steps. "Don't you think it's a terrific day? Don't you think this is a nice house? Look there— it's got a genuine brass kick plate on the front door. I really like that."

Michelle frowned, looking hard into his bright blue eyes. "Have you been drinking?"

"It's eleven o'clock in the morning," Thomas replied indignantly. "What a question to ask. Look at those lamps on either side of the door—they're brass, too."

"Thomas, what on earth are you—"

"Come with me," he said, opening his very own front door with a flourish. "I have something to show you."

He gave her the deluxe tour, starting from the ground floor and working his way up to the nursery on the top floor.

He talked faster and with more enthusiasm than Constance Lipman had ever dreamed of, pointing out everything from the breaker box to the linen closet to the crown molding. By the time they went back to the living room, he realized she hadn't said a word. Not a single word.

"So what do you think?" he asked finally, watching her for signs of life. She didn't move. She didn't blink. She just watched him with those big brown eyes that didn't give a thing away. He clicked his fingers in front of her nose. "Hello? Anybody in there?"

Michelle's face was pale. "Why am I here?"

"Why? Because I wanted to show you the house." He attempted to touch her, but she moved away. "What's wrong with you?"

"I saw the For Sale sign in the front yard," Michelle said tonelessly. In her heart she knew that there had to be a reasonable explanation for all this. There had to be.

"It's not for sale anymore."

"What . . . do you mean?"

"I mean I just bought it. Today. I signed the papers less than an hour ago." Now she would show some emotion, he thought. She would start jumping up and down and hugging him and crying for joy. Women were like that.

And she did show some emotion—but not quite what Thomas had hoped for. What was left of her color drained from her face. Her jaw dropped, her eyes stretched, her hands began to tremble. "You *bought* this house?"

This was not going according to plan. "I did," Thomas said, watching her carefully. Something about her expression reminded him of the night she had taken a swing at him. "You know, this isn't quite the reaction I had hoped for from you, Mick. You're making me a little nervous here."

"You don't want a house!"

"*Yes* I do." Thomas was beginning to get irritated. "I want *this* house. And in case you haven't noticed, this is the two-story colonial that you've been dreaming about all your life. There are big trees in the backyard so you can have tire swings. There's a white picket fence. It's everything you wanted, Mick!"

"So why did *you* buy it?" she demanded. "There isn't a palm tree in the whole yard, Thomas, not a beach in sight. This isn't what you've dreamed about all your life!"

"But it is, it's exactly what—"

"Well, I won't let you do it! You're not sacrificing *any-thing* for me. I'll have my dream someday, but I'll share it with someone who wants it just as badly as I do!" Frustration and hurt constricted in her throat, making her voice crack. "What do you think I am, a charity case? Do you think I want to spend the rest of my life feeling like your ball and chain?"

"Will you just let me talk for a minute?"

"I can't believe you did this." She pursed her lips and blew her bangs out of her stinging eyes. "What happened to your someday island? What happened to the man who loved adventure and excitement? Good Lord, Thomas, you've got a mortgage now. What were you thinking of?"

"You," he said softly.

"Don't blame this on me. I didn't ask you to make any sacrifices for me. I didn't want you to. All I ever wanted was for you to be happy."

"I am, cupcake."

"You won't be."

"Yes, I will."

"I'm going home." She tried to make it out the front door, but he caught her by the arm, swinging her around to face him. Incredibly, he was laughing.

"Never what I expect," he gasped out, eyes watering, shoulders shaking. "You *are* home, Mick. Don't you know that? Can't you feel it?"

She caught her bottom lip between her teeth, chewing viciously. "You've gone crazy. You poor man, you've gone crazy. You're going to have grub worms in your lawn. Your sinks will get clogged up and you'll have to paint the siding every year. Don't you understand? I don't want that blamed on me!"

"I won't blame the grub worms on you," he promised, still laughing. He tipped her head back to look into her glistening eyes. "Sweet Mick, there will never be another like you. I love you with all my heart. You make me happier than I ever thought it was possible to be. And my dearest love—" he paused to gently kiss the tip of her nose "—I would much, much rather live in a forever house than on a someday island."

"I don't know what to say," Michelle whispered. She looked around her, as if seeing the house for the first time. Home. She felt it welcome her, draw her in. Were there still happy endings, then?

She lifted her gaze and saw him smile at her. He didn't look like a frightened man. He didn't look like a man who needed saving from the consequences of his folly. He looked like a man who knew exactly what he was doing.

"Marry me," he said.

"There are *six bedrooms*, Thomas."

"Marry me soon, then." He picked up a strand of her hair and rubbed it between his fingers, contentment and pleasure lighting his eyes. "Think of it as an adventure."

"Will you still play your harmonica?" she whispered.

"Every day."

"Promise?"

Thomas laughed and lifted her off the ground, hoisting her in the air. He kissed her, his face curtained in her hair, her white ballet shoes standing tiptoe on his tennis shoes. "Cross my heart."

She looked down into his blue, blue eyes and a sweet rush of pleasure filled her veins. There was a promise of forever in those eyes. "I love you," she said. "I love you so much."

He lowered her to the ground slowly, his lips tasting her tears. "You can't cry," he said. "There aren't any tears allowed in our forever house."

She sniffled. "These are good tears. Happy tears."

He nodded, emotion crowding up in his chest and his throat, making it hard for him to speak. Miracles did that to a man.

"That's all right, then," he said softly, pulling her close. "That's all right."

The setting sun tinted him with fiery red and gold as he walked slowly to his car. It was an incredible evening, the colors of the sunset richer and brighter than any he'd seen on his tropical island travels. He threw back his head and began to laugh, lost in the wonder of a dream that had finally come true. It seemed that paradise was closer than he'd realized.

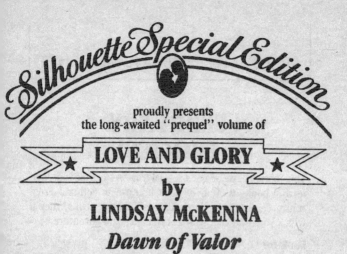

Silhouette Special Edition

proudly presents
the long-awaited "prequel" volume of

★ LOVE AND GLORY ★

by
LINDSAY McKENNA

Dawn of Valor

In the summer of '89, Silhouette Special Edition premiered three
novels celebrating America's men and women in uniform: LOVE
AND GLORY, by bestselling author Lindsay McKenna. Featured
were the proud Trayherns, a military family as bold and patriotic
as the American flag—three siblings valiantly battling the threat
of dishonor, determined to triumph... in love and glory.

Now, discover the roots of the Trayhern brand of courage, as
parents Chase and Rachel relive their earliest heartstopping
experiences of survival and indomitable love, in

Dawn of Valor, Silhouette Special Edition #649.

This February, experience the thrill of LOVE AND GLORY—from
the very beginning!

DV-1

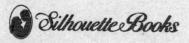

Silhouette Books

Take 4 bestselling love stories FREE

Plus get a FREE surprise gift!

Silhouette romances are now available in stores at these convenient times each month.

Silhouette Desire
Silhouette Romance

These two series will be in stores on the 4th of every month.

Silhouette Intimate Moments
Silhouette Special Edition

New titles for these series will be in stores on the 16th of every month.

We hope this new schedule is convenient for you. With only two trips each month to your local bookseller, you will always be sure not to miss any of your favorite authors!

Happy reading!

Please note there may be slight variations in on-sale dates in your area due to differences in shipping and handling.

**Star-crossed lovers?
Or a match made in heaven?**

Why are some heroes strong and
silent . . . and others charming
and cheerful? The answer is
WRITTEN IN THE STARS!

Coming each month in 1991,
Silhouette Romance presents
you with a special love story
written by one of your favorite
authors—highlighting the hero's
astrological sign! From January's
sensible Capricorn to December's
disarming Sagittarius, you'll
meet a dozen dazzling and
distinct heroes.

Twelve heavenly heroes . . . twelve
wonderful Silhouette Romances
destined to delight you. Look for
one WRITTEN IN THE STARS
title every month throughout
1991—only from Silhouette
Romance.   STAR

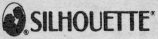